This is the last page of

SUPER MARIO™ MANGA MANIA

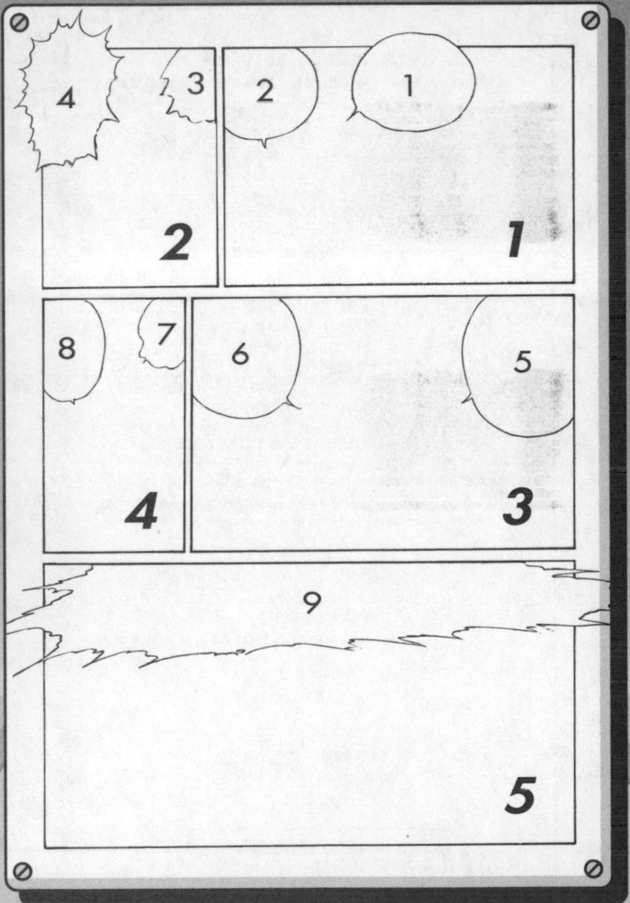

To properly enjoy this VIZ Media graphic novel, please turn it around and begin reading from right to left.

SUPER MARIO™
MANGA MANIA

VIZ MEDIA EDITION
STORY AND ART BY YUKIO SAWADA

Translation: Caleb Cook
English Adaptation: Molly Tanzer
Lettering: Vanessa Satone
Design: Adam Grano
Editor: Joel Enos

Printed in the U.S.A.

Published by VIZ Media, LLC
P.O. Box 77010
San Francisco, CA 94107

10 9 8 7 6 5 4 3 2 1
First printing, December 2020

viz.com

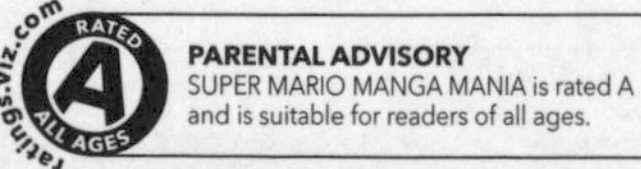

SUPER MARIO™

MANGA MANIA

Story and Art by

YUKIO SAWADA

SUPER MARIO™
MANGA MANIA

features stories that were handpicked especially for you by the manga's creator, Yukio Sawada. Some selections will make you laugh, some might make you cry, and all are the greatest hits from the long-running manga series known as *Super Mario-kun* in Japan.

TABLE OF CONTENTS

STAGE 1
Counting on You, Sushie!
(PAPER MARIO)
7

STAGE 2
The Super-Sad Red Coin Tale
(SUPER MARIO SUNSHINE)
23

STAGE 3
Off to Help the Squid Squad!
(SUPER MARIO SUNSHINE)
39

STAGE 4
Final Battle Against a Well-Armed Enemy!
(MARIO & LUIGI: PARTNERS IN TIME)
55

STAGE 5
Beat 'Em with Laughs! The Bros. Face Off in Space?!
(SUPER PAPER MARIO)
71

STAGE 6
Who's the Fourth Hero?!
(SUPER PAPER MARIO)
89

STAGE 7
Gag Battle at the Edge of Space!
(SUPER MARIO GALAXY)
105

STAGE 8
The Tale of Yoshi and Chain Chomp
(NEW SUPER MARIO BROS. Wii)
121

STAGE 9
Solve the Christmas Mystery!
(SUPER MARIO SUNSHINE)
136

NOTE FOR PARENTS: The stories in the following section have some sad material that may upset sensitive kids. Please use discretion when reading them aloud.

SPECIAL STAGE
Super Mari-*Old*
145

BONUS STAGE
Old Yukio Sawada's Super Secrets, Part 1
160

BONUS STAGE
Old Yukio Sawada's Super Secrets, Part 2
162

And Now, the Afterword
164

I GAVE THE ABOVE ILLUSTRATION to Kendo Kobayashi when I had the privilege of appearing on *Mandou Kobayashi*, which airs on satellite TV and other networks.

During the show, they told viewers how many times the words "poop" and "fart" showed up in the first 52 volumes of the Super Mario-kun series. Throughout those 686 chapters, "poop" appeared 119 times, and "fart" appeared 77 times.

Those numbers actually seem low, to me...

But don't worry. I tried to choose somewhat more... decent selections for this best-of collection. So (I'm sorry to say) you probably won't come across too many poops and farts.

—YUKIO SAWADA

STAGE 1
COUNTING ON YOU, SUSHIE!

*This chapter is based on the **Paper Mario** game, in which Mario, Goombario, Kooper and pals set out to rescue the seven Star Spirits and take back the Star Rod that Bowser stole.

THESE TRADING CARDS ARE PRETTY COOL...
HMM...
SORRY ABOUT THE WAIT.
KA-DUM
BUT NOT THE RIGHT KIND OF COOL, YOU DUMMY!
NEVER MIND!
MY STAR ROD CAN GRANT ANY WISH, SO...
EVEN THE STAR ROD'S OVER-HEATED...
WORMP~~
ICE CREAM, SHAVED ICE, CHILLED WATER-MELON... THIS'LL COOL ME DOWN!
Oh yeah.
LICK LICK
KRONCH KRONCH
PLEASED NOW, MY LORD?
RIGHT.
MEANWHILE, MARIO'S GANG MUST BE FEELING THE HEAT...

MT. LAVA-LAVA
STEE—M
STEE—M

WHEW!
ANOTHER HOT ZONE!
HOTTER THAN THE LAST...
URGHH!

HEAT LIKE THIS MAKES A GUY LOSE HIS APPETITE.
RIGHT, SUSHIE?
OH, I'M NOT HUNGRY AT ALL.

Hey! Shut up!
SUMMER IS AS HOT AS A VOLCANO IS BALD.
SO OF COURSE A VOLCANO IN SUMMER WOULD BE HOTTER THAN HECK!
Total nonsense
SUSHIE
PARTNER WHO JOINED THE PARTY IN YOSHI'S VILLAGE!
KRONCH
KRONCH
I JUST KNOW I'M LOSING WEIGHT...
YOU ARE NOT!
CRACKERZ
CHIPZ
LET'S-A-GO...
YEAH!
LET'S JUST FIND MISSTAR AND GET OUT OF HERE.
Misstar
OOH, BLOCKS!
LOOK, MARIO-BLOCKS!
LOOK AT THAT RIVER OF LAVA!
AND NO BRIDGE...
HOW DO WE CROSS IT?
Mm-hm!
AHA! I'VE GOT IT!

MAKE A BRIDGE WITH THE BLOCKS!!
THE BLOCKS, MAN!!
WHAT'S DONE IS DONE. RELAX!
HOW IS THIS BETTER?!
WE'LL USE KOOPER AS A BRIDGE!
Gah.
SO HOT. BOY, I'M THIRSTY!
SUSHIE SURE IS CHEER-FUL...
C'MON, LET'S GO!
JUST A MOMENT.
SPLOOSH
HERE, HAVE SOME NICE FRESH WATER!
OH, THANKS A LOT!
BLARGHH
GULP GULP
DELISH.
CAN I GET SOME TOO?

OLD YUKIO'S Mini SPECIAL NOTE

Luigi and Yoshi are Mario's constant companions.

In some games, however, those regulars step aside to make room for guest stars like the Red Bob-omb, or the baby Yoshis. *Paper Mario* has Goombario and Kooper, *Super Mario Sunshine* has F.L.U.D.D., and *Paper Mario: The Thousand Year Door* has Goombella and Koops. And of course, there's Baby Mario, Baby Luigi, Luma, Starlow, and so on and so forth. By the time an arc is over, we've all come to love those companions, so it's bittersweet when I have to draw them in the final chapters. Parting is always such sweet sorrow...

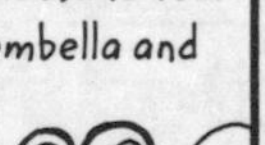

I am F.L.U.D.D. !!

WHERE DID YOU GET THAT "WATER"?

MY OWN PERSONAL STASH, OF COURSE!

CUT IT OUT!

SPLISH

IT COMES OUT THE OTHER END, TOO!

HUH ...

I ACTUALLY FEEL A LOT BETTER!

YEAH!

LET'S-A-GO-GO-GO!

LOOK AT MARIO GO!

PSST... IT'S ACTUALLY AN ENERGY DRINK.

TOMP-TOMP-TOMP

ROLL ROLL ROLL ROLL

EEK !

HUH ?!

ROLL ROLL ROLL
HELP ME!
LEAVE THIS CHUMP TO ME!
BWAH
MARIO'S BACK ALREADY!
KOOPER!
SPINY TROMP
WHAT'RE YOU SUPPOSED TO BE–A DUNG BEETLE?!
HRNNGH!
TMpTMp TM—p
ROLL ROLL ROLL ROLL
SWOOSH
GAHHH!
Argh...
I'M POOP-ED...
FWEW

THIS IS NO TIME FOR A SNACK ATTACK! HELP US!
KRONCH KRONCH
YESSS?
ROLL ROLL
SUSHIE!
IT'S COMING THIS WAY!
KA-BLAMMO
IF I MUST.
SKWISH
SQUIRT!
SKWERRT
YOU TROUNCED THAT TROMP!
FORGETTING SOMEONE?!
MOVING RIGHT ALONG...
WE CAN COUNT ON YOU, SUSHIE!
DON'T CALL ME THAT.
NOT BAD FOR AN OLD LADY!

WE'VE BEEN WALKING FOREVER.
WHERE COULD MISSTAR BE?
IS IT JUST ME, OR IS IT GETTING EVEN HOTTER?
BWO-OSH
BLECKHYUCKHYUCK!
THAT WOULD BE MY FAULT!
WAHH!
LAVA PIRANHA!
THAT'S THE BOSS OF THE VOLCANO...
WE CAN RESCUE MISSTAR IF WE BEAT IT!
FIRE PIRANHAS ARE WEAK TO SNOW...
...NO MATTER HOW BIG THEY ARE! SO...
LET'S USE THE RIGHT ITEM!

SWEAT~ SWEAT~
HUH ?!
SWEAT~ SWEAT~ SWEAT~ SWEAT~ SWEAT~
YOIKS !
BWAM
SNOW-MAN DOLL!
NICE MOVE, GOOMBARIO !
YOU USED KOOPER ?!
I'M MELTING IN HERE!!
ACK !
ZOOOP
Welp. That didn't work...
eeek!
HOT, HOT, HOT!
BWAH BWAH
CHOMP
NIPPER PLANTS, ATTACK !
BWAHBWAH
ENOUGH MESSING AROUND...

DANCE, DANCE, DANCE!
FIRE DANCE!
HEY, NO DANCING!
HA-CHA-CHA-CHA!
Nice moves...
SPLOO—SH
HELP!
eek!
SUSHIE'S MOVE: *WATER BLOCK*
THAT DID THE TRICK.
BLOOOP
Oh...
YOU GUYS'LL BE SAFE IN THERE...
...WHILE I BEAT THIS GUY!
AAHH!
SQUIRT!
BELLY FLOP!
BWOOMP
SPLURT
URRGH!

SPIN
ULP.
DON'T LEAVE THE WATER BLOCK!
NICE GOING, SUSHIE!
SPLISH
FWOOM
FLAME SPEW!
SUSHIE! NOOOO!
WOOSH
AHHH!
DON'T EVEN THINK ABOUT IT!
SMAK
...ALL BROILED AND ACTUALLY TASTY LOOKING!
YOU SAVED ME...AND NOW YOU'RE...
SIZZLE

...YOU GUYS HAVE NO CHOICE BUT TO RETIRE.
WITH SUSHIE OUT OF THE GAME...
BLECK HYUCK HYUCK YUCK!
HUH ?!
MY FINAL BIG MOVE...
MARIO... DON'T GIVE UP JUST YET...
DRAG DRAG
NOT THAT KIND OF RETIRE-MENT!
THIS SURE BEATS WORK-ING.
WHAT'S THAT HEART DOING THERE?
SMOOCHIE
SMOOCH
I'M GIVING IT TO YOU!
URK!
SMOOCH SMOOCH SMOOCH
URGHHH.
WHOOSH

YOU CAN DO IT, MARIO!
A MOUTHFUL OF ENERGY AND COURAGE!
BWOO~~MP
W-WHAT'S THIS NOW?
URP...
SMAK
Wahh!
Oh, I'm so nice and slim, now.
This is still Sushie
KABLOOOSH
AAAAHAHH!
TIDAL WAVE!
GOOD GOING, MARIO!

FIRE'S OUT. NICE.
SKWERRT
WELL DONE.
FZZL
BWOOMP
AFTER I JUST MANAGED TO SLIM DOWN.
EVEN TUBBIER THAN BEFORE!
BWAH
THANK YOU, MARIO.
MIS-STAR!
AND THANK YOU TOO, SUSHIE.
HERE'S MY HEALING SMOOCH!
SMOOCH
MEAN-WHILE...
GURGL GURGL
ARGH!
THIS WON'T BE PRETTY...
TOO MUCH COLD FOOD, LORD BOWSER?
... BOWSER WAS LOSING WEIGHT!

STAGE 2
THE SUPER-SAD RED COIN TALE

*This chapter is based on the **Super Mario Sunshine** game, in which the source of Isle Delfino's light—the Shine Sprites—have vanished due to the power of mysterious paint goop. Shadow Mario is also rumored to be lurking around the island, so Mario sets out on a new adventure with F.L.U.D.D. on his back.

SPLISH SPLISH SPLISH
WE CLEAN AND CLEAN, BUT THE MESS WON'T GO AWAY.
GLOOP

EEEP!
ROLL
ROLL ROLL
CUT THAT OUT!
GLOOP
...
SPIN

OR ELSE HE'S GONNA GET WASHED AWAY!!!
FSH

THAT IS A STROLLIN' STU.
HE'S GONNA STROLL AWAY IF HE KNOWS WHAT'S GOOD FOR HIM!

UM. WE DIDN'T BLAST YOU YET...
FWUMP

URGH ...
SOMETHING IS WRONG WITH HIM.
CLK CLK
SNAP OUT OF IT, STU!
SPLOOSH
ACK!
SPRAYING HIM WITH WATER WILL NOT IMPROVE HIS CONDITION!

WHAT'S GOING ON?
I'VE BEEN SO STRESSED-STU. I'M ON MY LAST LEGS-STU.

MY SISTER IS VERY SICK-STU... I'M UP ALL NIGHT TO CARE FOR HER-STU...

I'M SOOO TIRED-STU...

BUT I'VE GOT MY DAY JOB-STU. NO VACATION DAYS ALLOWED-STU.

IS WHAT YOU DO SO SPECIAL?

WHAT IS YOUR JOB, EXACTLY?

TO COVER THIS TOWN IN PAINT AND MAKE A BIG MESS-STU.

THAT'S NO WAY TO MAKE A LIVING!

MY SISTER AND I ARE DONE FOR AT THIS RATE-STU, BUT...
YOU'RE IN DEAD LAST!
BIANCO HILLS MESS-MAKING RANKINGS
Strollin' Stu
Pokey
Swoopin' Stu
Piranha Plant
Gatek
Seec
I HAVEN'T BEEN HITTING MY QUOTA, RECENTLY-STU...
WHY TELL ME ABOUT IT...?
BUT I CAN'T DO IT-STU...
THERE ARE EIGHT RED COINS IN THIS TOWN. COLLECTING THEM COULD CURE MY SISTER OF HER SICKNESS-STU.
FORGET THIS LOSER!
BUT... MARIO...
MY SISTER IS A BEAUTY WHO WON THE MISS BIANCO HILLS CONTEST-STU.
WHY'M I ALL WET?!
GUSH GUSH GUSH GUSH
WAHHH!
WHAT A SAD STORY!
SINCE WHEN CAN YOU CRY?!
I FEEL SO BAD FOR THE ILL SISTER!
WAHHH
WAHHH

SO, YOU WERE SAYING? I JUST HAVE TO COLLECT THE EIGHT RED COINS?
YOU ONLY CARE ABOUT THE GOOD-LOOKING SISTER!
THUMP
I'VE GOT THIS, DON'T WORRY.
YOU JUST SIT BACK AND RELAX!
FSH
MARIO, IT'S IN YOUR HANDS-STU...
HEY F.L.U.D.D., YOU MUST KNOW WHERE THOSE RED COINS ARE, RIGHT?
NATURALLY. I AM AN EXCEPTIONAL APPLIANCE.
ENOUGH ADVERTISING-JUST TELL ME ALREADY.
THE FIRST IS ATOP THE WALL.
GOT IT!
JUST AHEAD IS...
HUH?
...A *FAKE* COIN. WE DO NOT REQUIRE THAT ONE.
TOOK YOU LONG ENOUGH TO MENTION!
FAKE

For this greatest-hits collection, it was a real challenge to choose just eight or nine out of almost 700 chapters across 52 volumes. The Baby Yoshi story is one of my favorites, but it had to be cut because there wasn't room in the book. Personally, I'm a fan of the stories where Mario **doesn't** appear.

For instance, he doesn't show up in Stage 7 of volume 27 or Special Stage 1 of volume 29, but he's still pivotal to the story.

Then, on a slightly different note, you have ones like Stage 10 of volume 40, which puts the spotlight on Bowser and the Goombas.

If the chance arises, I'd like to include those sorts of stories in a future volume of *Super Mario Manga Mania!*

Yello, friends!
Starlow

THAT'S TWO COINS!
AND THREE!!
EASY-PEASY. WHERE'S NUMBER FOUR?
THE NEXT COIN IS...

...UP THERE.
SPARKL
TOO HIGH!

I CAN'T JUMP THAT HIGH!
A BOOST FROM MY ROCKET NOZZLE WILL SUFFICE.
LET'S SWAP TO YOUR ROCKET NOZZLE!
OH YEAH!
ROGER!

WHAP
NICE RETURN, F.L.U.D.D.!!
IT'S GOTTA BE ROCKET NOZZLE!
...WAIT. NOT RACKET NOZZLE !!
ROCKET-DOODLE-DOO!
ENOUGH OF THAT, YOU BIRD-BRAIN!
THESE GAGS HAVE GOTTA STOP!
↑ Whose feet are these ?
← Again, who is this?!
ROCKET NOZZLE: SUPER JUMP!
ZOOOOOOSH
GOT THE FOURTH COIN!
MARIO AND F.L.U.D.D. KEPT GRABBING RED COINS.
FOUND THE FIFTH ONE!
WHOOSH

WHA—m
WAH!
YOU JUMPED TOO FAR.

BONK
SIXTH ONE.
NGAH~!

BOI~NG
SEVENTH.
GRAP

IT WAS A SIMPLE, EASY TASK.
AHHH!
FWISH—
SLAM
DOESN'T LOOK EASY TO ME!
← Seriously, who are you?!

YOU HAVE MANAGED TO COLLECT SEVEN OF THEM.
BUT YOU ARE LOOKING WORSE FOR WEAR, MARIO.
WORMP~
LIFE

JUST ONE MORE, RIGHT?
WHERE IS IT, EXACTLY?
HERE
YOU NEED ONLY TO CROSS THIS ROPE.

IT'LL TAKE THE LAST OF MY STRENGTH...

KZZT
KZZT
KZZT
PLEASE BE CAREFUL, AS YOU WILL ENCOUNTER A WIRE TRAP ON THE WAY.
TOO LITTLE ...
KZZT
KZZT
LIFE
WIRE TRAP
WATER DOES NOT DESTROY WIRE TRAPS.
DO SOMETHING ABOUT THAT FOR ME.
KZZT
KZZT
...TOO LATE!
ARGHH ...
STAY BACK.
BACK, YOU.
CREEP
KZZT
KZZT
KZZT
AHHH !
WHAP
YOU MUST TAKE THE DIRECT APPROACH!

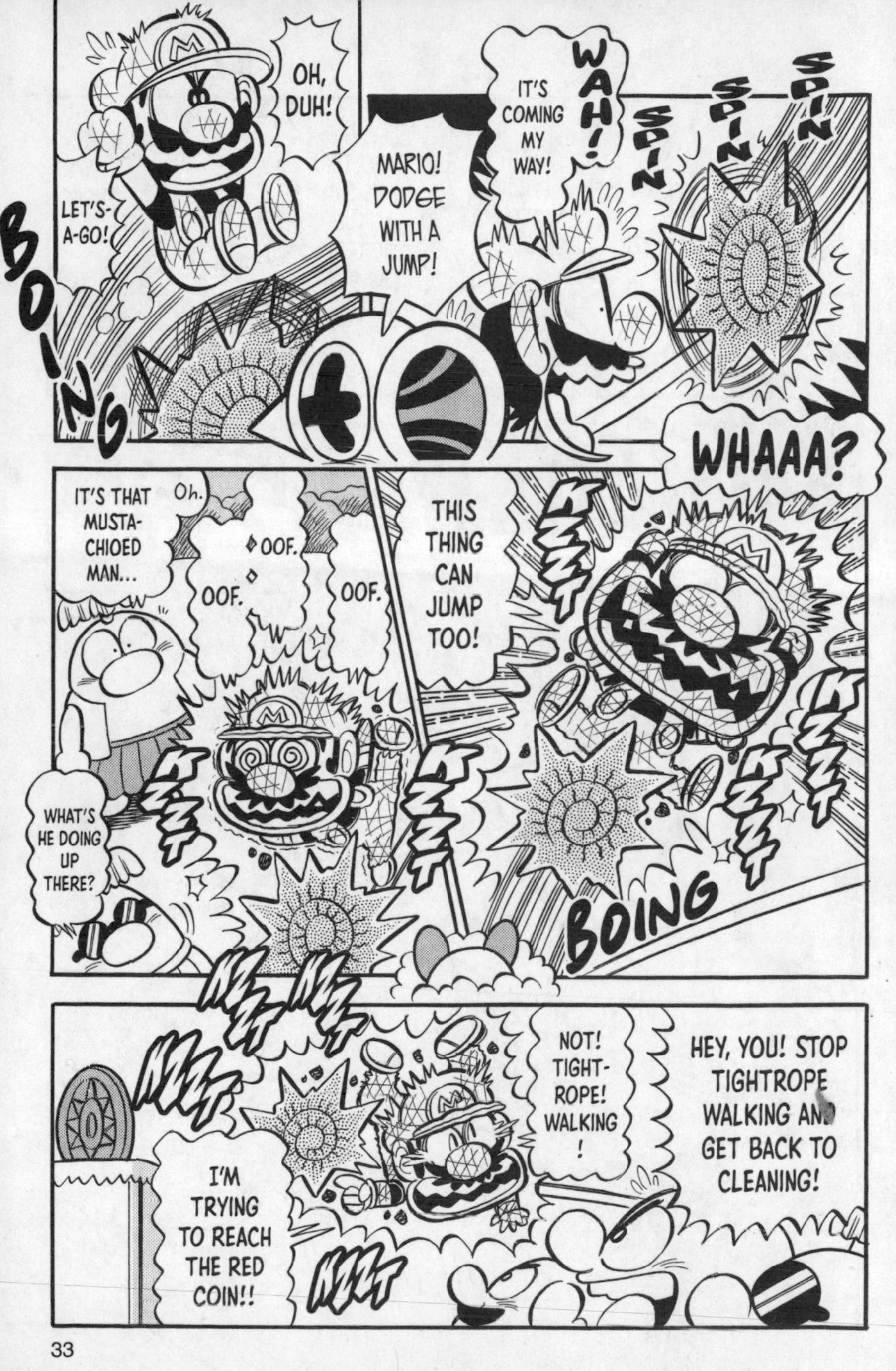
OH, DUH!
LET'S-A-GO!
BOING
MARIO! DODGE WITH A JUMP!
IT'S COMING MY WAY!
WAH!
SPIN
SPIN
SPIN
WHAAA?
IT'S THAT MUSTACHIOED MAN...
Oh.
OOF.
OOF.
OOF.
THIS THING CAN JUMP TOO!
WHAT'S HE DOING UP THERE?
BOING
HEY, YOU! STOP TIGHTROPE WALKING AND GET BACK TO CLEANING!
NOT! TIGHT-ROPE! WALKING!
I'M TRYING TO REACH THE RED COIN!!

WHY WOULD YOU HELP A GUY WHO'S DIRTYING UP OUR TOWN?
STU? THAT ROUND LITTLE BADDIE?
... STROLLIN' STU'S SICK LITTLE SISTER CAN GET BETTER.
ONCE I HAVE THEM ALL...
KNNT
KNNT
KNNT
YOU JERKS!
FRIEND? BADDIE? DOESN'T MATTER WHEN SOMEONE'S IN TROUBLE!
...SO MARIO WAS EAGER TO HELP ...
THE SISTER IN QUESTION IS SUPPOSEDLY ATTRACTIVE...
KNNT
KNNT
KNNT
NOPE! CAN'T DO IT!
I HAVE TO BEAT THIS CHALLENGE ...
I'M DOING THIS!

WAHHH!
KZZZT
KZZZT
NAA AAH HH!
KZZZT
KZZZT
KZZZT
YEAH. REALLY, REALLY DUMB.
WHAT A DUMMY ...
GOING TO ALL THAT TROUBLE FOR AN ENEMY...
FSS——H
WE'VE GOT NO CHOICE ...
WE CAN'T STAND BACK AND WATCH!
NO. NOTHING DUMB ABOUT IT!
NAB THAT RED COIN!
KZZZT
KZZZT
NOW'S YOUR CHANCE ...
WE'RE HERE TO HELP!
THANKS A LOT, GUYS!
KZZZT
HEY, STU!

MARIO !!
THUD
DID SOMEONE ORDER A BUNCH OF RED COINS?!
LIFE 5
BEEP BEEP BEEP
THANKS, BUD.
YOU'VE REALLY DONE ME A SOLID...
YEAH. WONDER-FUL...
HOW WONDER-FUL.
NOW YOUR BEAUTIFUL SISTER WILL BE FINE...
YOUR SISTER? HER BEAUTY? HER SICKNESS...?
...
EXCEPT... YOU DUMMY!
IT WAS ALL A LIE FROM THE START!
I TRICKED YOU, MARIO!
YOUR PLAN WENT PERFECTLY, BROTHER!
NAW, I DO HAVE A SISTER, BUT SHE'S DOING FINE!
SHE WON A BEAUTY CONTEST?
THUD

MY PLAN WAS TO HAVE YOU WEAR YOURSELF OUT GATHERING COINS, AND THEN—KA-POW—I'D GETCHA.
AND WITH THOSE RED COINS, I'D RISE IN THE RANK-INGS!!
WAH HAHA HAHA
TRUSTING A BADDIE? HOW DUMB AM I?
OH NO!
SLUMP
EXCEPT... YOU DOOFUS!
THOSE COINS ARE ALL FAKES!
THE REAL RED COINS ARE OVER HERE!
DOOOM
ALL YOU'VE GOT ARE TOMATO SLICES.
A SWITCH-EROO? BUT WHEN, MARIO ...?
ARGHH!
SKWOO~~SH
YOU'RE STILL ALL BEATEN UP!
WEAK ENOUGH FOR ME TO TAKE YOU OUT!
NOPE.
BECAUSE THESE REAL RED COINS...
HUH ?!
BWAH
FSH

BWUH!
KAPOW
LIFE
CAN BOOST ME BACK TO FULL HEALTH!
ALL THAT PAIN YOU PUT US THROUGH, FOR NOTHING!
WHO GETS TRICKED SO EASILY, HUH?!
YOU LOSER.
YOU THOUGHT YOU COULD FOOL ME?
WHAP
BOP
EEK! I'M SOOORRY!!
LOO—M
HUH?!
SPEAKING OF LOSERS...
THAT'S NOT GONNA WORK AGAIN!
OUR GORGEOUS BIG SISTER TOO...
MY LOVELY MOTHER IS ILL...

STAGE 3
OFF TO HELP THE SQUID SQUAD!

*This chapter is also based on the **Super Mario Sunshine** game.

HERE YOU ARE, PRINCESS.
MY BANANA PLEASE, TOADSWORTH.
THAT'S JUST AN (IN)HUMAN-PYRAMID!
THAT IS MUCH BETTER.
OKAAAAY.
ZWOO—SH
KADUM
GET IN THERE ALREADY!
WHERE ARE WE ...?!
RICO HARBOR.
THE LARGEST PORT TOWN ON THE ISLAND.
THAT EXPLAINS ALL THE FISH.
Fish, fish fish

...THOSE FISH AREN'T SAFE FOR EATING.
NOW THAT THE HARBOR'S ALL COVERED IN GOOP...

HUH ?!
YOU CAN'T EAT THOSE FISH!
Hey!

NOT SUR-PRISED...
ARE YOU LISTEN-ING?!
MUNCH
MUNCH
YUM, YUM!

LET US INVESTIGATE THIS, MARIO.
WELL, YOU HAVE THE SAME MUSTACHE, SO I'M HOLDING YOU RESPONSIBLE.
SURE, SURE.

...
...
THERE'S BEEN SO MUCH TROUBLE AT THE HARBOR EVER SINCE THAT MUSTACHIOED MAN IN A HAT SHOWED UP...
IT'S YOU, ISN'T IT!
NO WAY!
BUT I SEE HOW YOU COULD MAKE THAT MISTAKE...

ZRM ZRM ZRM

WHERE'S THAT SHADOWY IMPOSTOR ...?
THIS BOAT'S ALL COVERED IN GOOP, TOO.

REVENGE FOR MOM!
EAT THIS!
MUS-TACHE MAN!
SPLORT
AAHHH!

FWAHH!
KA-SPLOOSH
THAT'S NOT ENOUGH TO KEEP ME DOWN!
WE DID IT!
THE MUSTACHE MAN IS DEFEATED!
HOORAY! HOORAY!
FWUMP

SAY IT, DON'T SPRAY IT!
SPLORT
HEY, YOU'RE RIGHT.
OH—LOOK. WE GOT THE WRONG GUY.
STARE
ANYWAY, WHAT DO YOU MEAN? REVENGE FOR MOM?
OUR MOM WAS ALWAYS THE NICEST...
I DREW A PICTURE OF YOU, MOMMY.
AND I WROTE AN ESSAY.
LET ME SEE.
...OUR MOM HAS BECOME MEAN AND VIOLENT.
EVER SINCE THIS GUY WHO LOOKS LIKE YOU CAME TO THE HARBOR...
I'M NOT THIS UGLY, YEESH!
AND THIS ESSAY IS GARBAGE!
WHAP
NOT EXACTLY PROVING YOUR POINT, HERE.
THE IMPOSTOR IS AT IT AGAIN, IT SEEMS.
YEP.
SHE'S JUST REAL STRONG, THAT'S ALL!
SHE'S A GREAT MOM THOUGH, WE PROMISE!
SURE, OKAY.
JUST TAKE US TO YOUR MOM, OKAY?

HERE.
THESE ARE STACKS OF CONTAINERS.
AH.
THAT'S MOM'S LEG!
THIS HUGE THING?!
ALL RIGHT, EVERYONE PULL.
WE'LL DRAG HER OUT.
HEAVE-HO!
OKAY!
BWAHH!
YOU DIDN'T SAY WHAT WE WERE PULLING!
THE LEG, OBVIOUSLY!
OKAY!
NOT MY LEG, YOU JERK!
UGH!
WOR~~MP
NOW PULL!
ONE, TWO...
THREE———!!
HNNGH

ZABWAM
GOOPER BLOOPER
SQUID-
MONGOUS
!
MOM
!

WHAP
WWHAPP
GAH!
RUB RUB
EHHH?!
WHO BEATS UP THEIR OWN KIDS, YOU BRUTE?!
FSH
LOOKS LIKE A BUNCHA GRAPES.
YIKES!
LITTLE ROUGH, MOM.
PLOOMP
AND MARIO'S A TOMATO, NOW.
AHHHH
AAH!
GOOPER BLOOPER ISN'T ANYONE'S MAMA ANYMORE!
MWA HA HA HA HA HA!
SMAK SMAK SMAK
BWAHHH~!

GET THEM, GOOPER BLOOPER!
I KNEW IT! YOU'RE TO BLAME FOR ALL THIS!
SHE'S MY LOYAL SERVANT!
SMAK
SMAK
SMAK
AAH!
WAHH!
OUR MOM WASN'T ALWAYS LIKE THIS...
IT'S ALL CUZ OF THAT GOOP ON HER FACE.
MARIO! I HAVE A FEELING THAT GOOP IS THE CAUSE OF THIS!
SO WE JUST GOTTA WIPE OFF THAT BAD MAKEUP JOB?

SHE BLOCKED IT?!
FWP
SPLISH
SPLISH SPLISH
SQUIRT AWAY, F.L.U.D.D.!
ROGER!
FWP
WE'RE NOT PLAYING PEEK-A-BOO HERE!
DOOM
CRUD.
IT IS NO USE.
GOTTA DO SOMETHING ABOUT THOSE TENTACLES.
WHAP
ACK!
MOM'S LEGS AREN'T DETACH-ABLE!
HOW ABOUT WE PULL IT RIGHT OFF!
GAH!

YAH!
WHAP
WHAP
WHAP
DO YOU WANT YOUR MOM BACK TO NORMAL OR NOT?!
YOU'RE HURTING HER!
Stop!
IF YOU DON'T STOP ARGUING, *WE'LL* BE HURTING!
HAP
I'M TEARING THIS THING OFF!
HRRNNGH!!
POP
SEEMS LIKE MOM...
...DOESN'T REMEMBER US...
SQUISHED SQUID
HOORAY!
MegaLuck
THIS IS SURE TO BE A LUCKY YEAR FOR ME!
THAT'S NOT A FORTUNE!

HRMPH!
I'LL PULL THIS ONE OUT TOO!
WOW, MISTER ...
THAT DIDN'T WORK!
S-S MMAAKK
WH-AP WH-AP
WHY YOU...
FWSH
SLAM
ACK!
WE WANT OUR MOM BACK!
YEAH!
WE HAVE TO HELP!
HEAVE, HO! HEAVE, HO!
PULL!
URK URK
NOOOO!!
POP
SOME-THING ELSE FELL OUT.
WE DID IT!
FLAP
FLAP

IT'S THE PICTURE I DREW OF MOM!
AND HERE'S MY ESSAY!
SHE WAS HANGING ON TO THESE ALL ALONG.
I GUESS THIS MEANS...
...SHE DIDN'T FORGET US AFTER ALL!
"I LOVE MY MOM."
"SHE'S SO NICE BUT ALSO REALLY STRONG, AND..."
MOVED
NOW IS OUR CHANCE, MARIO!
TO WASH AWAY...
...THE GOOP ON HER FACE!
KA-SPLOOSH
ENNGH!!

WHAT A HAPPY ENDING.
SPARKL SPARKL
SPARKL SPARKL
MM-HMM.
SORRY, EVERYONE.
AWW, MOM!
MOMMY!
POOF

GO AHEAD. ENJOY YOUR VICTORY FOR NOW.
I'M ONLY JUST GETTING STARTED...
I CAN DO YOUR MAKE-UP MUCH BETTER THAN THAT OTHER GUY.
THIS SOMEHOW SEEMS WORSE...

RAAWR!

GET READY FOR ROUND TWO!

BIG OCTOPUS!

WGGL WGGL

AKASHI OCTOPUS: JAPAN'S BEST

IF IT'S OCTOPUS YOU WANT, AKASHI'S THE PLACE TO FISH!

Celebrate 30 YEARS OF COROCORO MAGAZINE

GRILL ME UP AND EAT ME AND I'M SURE TO BE DELISH.

*This chapter is based on the **Mario & Luigi: Partners in Time** game, in which Mario and Luigi travel to the past in order to save Princess Peach. To do so, they must team up with their baby selves to oppose mysterious extraterrestrial invaders—the Shroobs!

FSH
MAYBE IF WE ALL BAND TOGETHER ...
MY TENTACLES CAN'T BE BEAT!
... YOU'LL STILL LOSE!
SMAK
WHAMMO
AAHH!
eek!

I SAID, TENTA-CLES!
GET IT?
WHAP
OH YEAH? I'LL GIVE YOU TEN TICKLES...
HUH ?
WGGL
WGGL

PRIN-
CESS
POKE!
OOF!
SHNK
YIKES!
ARGH!
SHNK
SHNK

LUIGI
TWIRL
!!
YOU
BETTER
NOT,
EITHER!
ENOUGH
OF
THAT!
SMAK
HIYAHH!
AHH!
eeek!

PRIN-
CESS
TWIRL
!
WHRRL
WHAP
eep!
WHRRL
MARIO
!
WHAP
WHAP
eep!
WHAP

THE NEXT
TENTACLE
ATTACK
IS GONNA
END US...
SHE'S
TOO
WELL-
ARMED.
UGH.
HAD
ENOUGH
?!

THE ATTACK MISSED!
PHEW
SMAK
HERE IT COMES! GOODBYE WORLD!
SWIG
EEEP.
ONLY ROOM FOR ONE PRINCESS IN THIS WORLD!
YOU'RE GONNA FEEL THE POKE TOO!
NOOOO!
NO MISS! IT'S HITTING PRINCESS PEACH!
SMAK
SMAK
EEK!
SMAK
SMSMAK
I PROTECT PRINCESS!
BABY MARIO!
WOOSH
HUH?!
PRIN-
FS—H

YOUR CHANCE... ATTACK MONSTER!
RIGHT!
OLD ME!
AWW... BABY MARIO! THANK YOU!
SMAK
I... ALWAYS... PROTECT YOU, PRINCESS PEACH!
SMAK
HOW CONFI-DENT!
I'LL BE THE ONE TO BEAT THIS BADDIE!
ON IT!
BOING
KA-POK POK POK
JUST KIDDING! THAT WON'T TAKE ME DOWN!
SMAK
TOO BAD FOR YOU, I'VE GOT MORE THAN ONE TENTACLE!
ARGHH.
POW POW POW
ANNOY-ING PESTS...
AAHHH!

HOW ABOUT THE WORST HUG YOU EVER HAD!
EHH!
AAHH!
EEK!
GRA—P
SKWEEZ
I MEANT FOR US! THAT MEDICINE PATCH WILL JUST GIVE HER A BOOST!
THERE! PAIN RELIEF FOR HER! ♡
AHH, IT'S WORKING WONDERS.
SKWEEZ
SOME-BODY STOP THE PAIN!
EEP!
HIC HIC
SEE? EVEN TIGHTER THAN BEFORE!
AAHH!
SKWEEZ
THIS COULD WORK ...
SLAP

WA—H WA—H

WA—H

NOOOO!!

OH NO...

WE DONE FOR!

I TOO YOUNG TO DIE!

SZZL

AAH! THAT HURTS!

HUH?! DID SHE SAY... THAT HURT?

PLIP PLIP

THIS MONSTER IS WEAK TO THE TEARS OF SWEET, INNOCENT BABIES!

IT MUST BE BABY TEARS!

TEARS ...?

SHE'S WEAK TO TEARS ?!

SKWIRT

LEMME TRY.

YOUR TEARS SEEM TO BE HEALING HER, ACTUALLY.

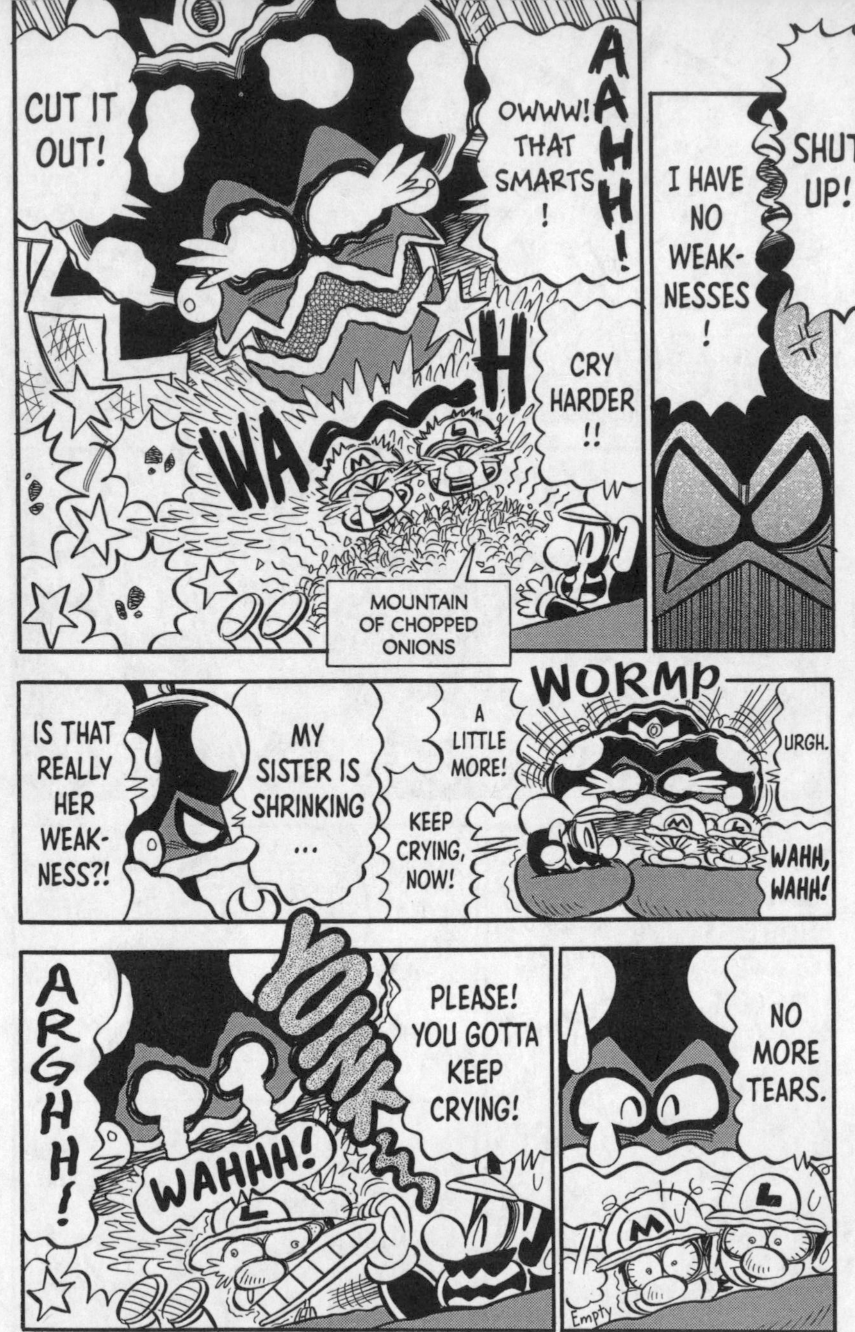
CUT IT OUT!
OWWW! THAT SMARTS!
AAHHH!
WA-H
CRY HARDER!!
MOUNTAIN OF CHOPPED ONIONS
I HAVE NO WEAK-NESSES!
SHUT UP!
IS THAT REALLY HER WEAK-NESS?!
MY SISTER IS SHRINKING...
A LITTLE MORE!
KEEP CRYING, NOW!
WORMP
URGH.
WAHH, WAHH!
ARGHH!
YOINK
WAHHH!
PLEASE! YOU GOTTA KEEP CRYING!
NO MORE TEARS.
Empty

HFF
HFF
HFF
YOU'RE NOT OUT OF THE WOODS YET.
WE'RE FREE!
YOU MAY HAVE ESCAPED MY TENTACLES...
FWAP
UGH.
THUD
WH-AP
SMAK
AAHHH!
...BUT I'VE STILL GOT THE POWER TO BEAT YOU!
HUH ?!
HERE–TRY USING THIS!
SPARKL
EHH ?!
PLEASE, POWERS THAT BE!
GIVE US THE STRENGTH WE NEED!
THIS TIME, I'LL MAKE SURE YOU ALL STAY DOWN!
WHAP
WHAP
Eek!
Ahh!
WHAP
Fwahh!

TA-DAH!
HUH?
A STAR SHELL !!
WHAA
MARIO & LUIGI INVINCIBLE BROS. ATTACK !!
OH, THANK YOU!
I'M SO GRATE-FUL!
EEP.
NOW GO, MARIO!
UAAAAH!!

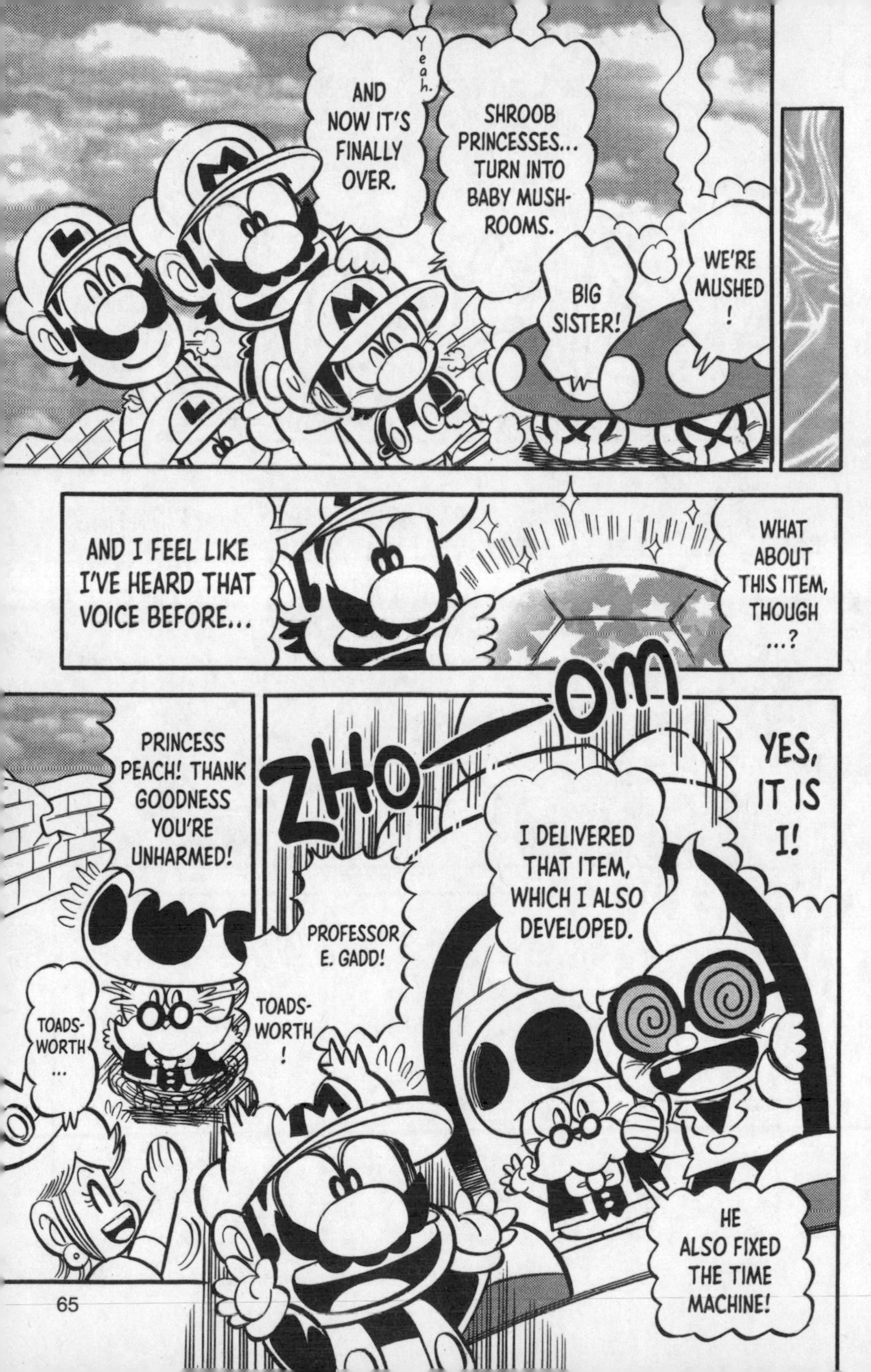
Yeah.
AND NOW IT'S FINALLY OVER.
SHROOB PRINCESSES... TURN INTO BABY MUSH-ROOMS.
WE'RE MUSHED!
BIG SISTER!
WHAT ABOUT THIS ITEM, THOUGH ...?
AND I FEEL LIKE I'VE HEARD THAT VOICE BEFORE...
ZHO—OM
YES, IT IS I!
I DELIVERED THAT ITEM, WHICH I ALSO DEVELOPED.
PROFESSOR E. GADD!
PRINCESS PEACH! THANK GOODNESS YOU'RE UNHARMED!
TOADS-WORTH!
TOADS-WORTH ...
HE ALSO FIXED THE TIME MACHINE!

OLD ME... THANK YOU!
EXCELLENT WORK, MARIO AND LUIGI...
YOU CAN'T REMAIN IN THIS ERA TOO LONG, AFTER ALL.
IT MIGHT END UP CHANGING HISTORY FOREVER.
AND NOW, IT'S TIME TO GO HOME.

AWW, BABY MARIO!
I'M PROUD THAT I'M YOU WHEN I GROW UP!
FIGHTING WAS LOTS OF FUN.

VRR—RM VRR—RM
ALL RIGHT, WE GOTTA GET BACK TO THE FUTURE.
BE WELL.
OKAY, OLD US!
ME TOO, ME TOO! THANKS!
BOW BOW BOW BOW BOW
YOU'RE VERY WEL-COME.

VO-OM
FAREWELL!
BYE-BYE.
Bye...
...
EVEN THOUGH WE SAID BYE TO OURSELVES...
AND EVEN THOUGH WE'LL MEET AGAIN...

WE CAN'T STOP CRYING...

WAHH WAHH

VOO—OM
I CAN'T EITHER.
SAME...
THE TIME MACHINE RETURNED.
WAHH
WAHH
OLD US!
BABIES...!
WAHH

SPECIAL THANKS TO S.TODAKA H.TOKUNAGA & KOCHIMU

THE BABIES' TEARS FELL LIKE RAIN...
FSH— FSH—
FSH—

...WASHING AWAY THE FOUL SHROOB INFESTATION THAT COVERED THE WORLD OF THE PAST...

HIP-HIP-HOORAY!

...AND RETURNING THE BEAUTIFUL, SHINING MUSHROOM KINGDOM...

...TO ITS FORMER GLORY...

WE'LL MEET AGAIN SOME-DAY.

STAGE 5
BEAT 'EM WITH LAUGHS! THE BROS. FACE OFF IN SPACE?!

*This chapter is based on the **Super Paper Mario** game, in which Mario sets out to gather the eight Pure Hearts with the help of Tippi and the other Pixls' mysterious powers, all to stop Count Bleck from destroying every world.

IS THAT ALL...? GOT IT!
WE'RE GATHERING THE PURE HEARTS TO STOP COUNT BLECK, WHO'S ATTEMPTING TO DESTROY ALL THE WORLDS.
Pure Heart(s)
Count Bleck
WAIT. WHAT ARE WE DOING AGAIN?
MAYBE YOU SHOULD'VE STAYED HOME, ACTUALLY!

JUST WATCH—I'LL BE THE ONE TO SAVE PEACH!

NOBODY MENTIONED HER!

A... URK... AH! UGHH HH! HH HH~

WHAT'S WRONG NOW, BOWSER?

CAN'T! BREATHE !!

I JUST REALIZED— WE'RE IN SPACE!

TOOK YOU LONG ENOUGH!

LET'S GIVE YOU A HELMET.

CWOP

THANKS! I LIVE ANOTHER DAY!

AND I'M READY TO HIT SOME HOME RUNS!
SWING
SWING

HOW'S A BASEBALL HELMET S'POSED TO HELP?!
HOW ABOUT THIS ONE...?

IT'S NOT ABOUT THE TEAM!
GIMME ONE LIKE YOURS!
OH. RIGHT.

AHHH.
THAT'S BETTER.
LET'S GET GOING!

THIS WAY...
LET'S GET GOING.
OKAY.

TIPPI, CAN YOU FEEL THE PURE HEART'S PRESENCE?
YES! I'M SENSING SOME-THING BIG.

CASTLE BLECK
NASTASIA, WHERE ARE YOU PLANT-ED?
NASTASIA
RIGHT HERE. WHAT IS IT, COUNT?
THAT'S NOT WHAT COUNT BLECK MEANT BY PLANTED!
MY MINIONS CONTINUE TO FALL TO THE HEROES, REMARKED COUNT BLECK.
TOTALLY! BUT THE HEROES ARE IN, LIKE, OUTER SPACE THIS TIME AROUND...
WELL, ARE THEY IN SPACE OR OUT OF IT?
OMG, NOW WHO'S PUNNING, COUNT?!
OUTER SPACE...
THEN THEY'RE SURE TO ENCOUNTER A CERTAIN MAN, REBORN...
THE MAN MORE SUITED TO GREEN THAN ANY GRASSHOPPER OR PICKLE...
THE GREEN THUNDER!!
THE ONE IN RED SHALL SOON LEARN...
BWAHAHAHAHAHAHA!

IT'S THE WHOA ZONE IN THERE, RIGHT?
I CAN SENSE THE PURE HEART BEYOND THIS GATE.

YOU HAVE THE KEY, BOWSER ?
I'VE GOT THIS.

THAT'S THE KEYHOLE, IN THAT PILLAR.
WE DON'T HAVE A KEY SHAPED LIKE THAT.

NOPE, BUT IF WE NEED A KEY...
GRAP
HUH ?!
KRAK KRIK
AAHH !
KRIK

KACH-AK
PERFECT FIT.
eek!

...WE JUST GOTTA MAKE ONE.
I'M NO KEY!
BAm

RRRRMBL
THE GATE IS OPENING.

BEHOLD THE GREEN THUNDER, MR. L!
SAY WHAT?!
HUH ?!
DON'T BE SILLY, LUIGI. WHAT'S WITH THAT GOOFY GETUP?!
I KNOW NOT OF THIS "LUIGI."
EXCEPT... YOU'RE CLEARLY LUIGI.

AAHH!
KA-POW
UNHAND ME!
ZOOP
...TO DESTROY ANY WHO DARE APPROACH IT!
KNOCK IT OFF ALREADY, LUIGI.
I AM NOT LUIGI.
THE NAME IS MR. L!
HA HA P
WAHH!
YOU'RE AFTER THIS PURE HEART, ARE YOU NOT?
WELL I'VE BEEN ORDERED BY COUNT BLECK HIMSELF ...
I'M SENSING EVIL ENERGY FROM LUIGI...
HE'S DEFINITELY BEEN BRAIN-WASHED BY DARKNESS.
BWOOM...

HMPH.
I'LL GET HIM BACK TO NORMAL!
LUIGI SEEMS TO HAVE A BAD CASE OF AMNESIA.
WAHH!
GO-NG
WAKE THE HECK UP, LUIGI!
YECH! STOP IT!
RUB RUB RUB
WELL HOW ABOUT THIS!
YOU'RE AFTER THIS PURE HEART, CORRECT?
YOU FOUL, STINKING, MUSTACHIOED FELLOW!
HOW DARE YOU, FOOL!
WHAM WHAM WHAM WHAM
WAHH!
HE'S A CHANGED MAN, FOR SURE!
WE'LL HAVE TO FIGHT HIM TO CLAIM IT...
BUT IT'LL BE TOUGH FOR MARIO...
...TO BATTLE HIS LITTLE BRO...

LUIGI, YOU JERK!
TAKE THIS AND THIS AND THIS!
GIMME THAT PURE HEART!
Never!
BOP BOP BOP BOP BOP
NOT TOO TOUGH, APPARENTLY.
WOMP WOMP
AS I SAID, I AM NOT LUIGI, YOU HAIRY-LIPPED FELLOW!
WHAK
Wahh!
THIS NEW LUIGI SEEMS TO BE STRONGER.
DID... DID YOU REALLY FORGET EVERYTHING?
ABOUT US...?
...
ALL THOSE FOND MEMORIES ...
KZZT
KZZT
AAHH!
KZZT FWP
UHH?
Yowwch!
SHU—NK
NOTHING FOND ABOUT THOSE MEMORIES FOR LUIGI!

RMMMMMBL
HUH ?!
UM...
COME TO ME, METAL BRO!
I'M FEEL-ING EXTRA ANGRY, FOR SOME REASON ...
BROBOT, DEPLOY!
A BATTLE-READY ROBOT?!
WHAT THE ?!
HUH ...
WHAT'S COMING OUT OF ITS NOSE?
FWSP
POP

KABOOM
CHEW ON THIS!
PEW PEW PEW PEW
MISSILES? REALLY?!
WAHH~~!
TCH. SO YOU WANNA PLAY DIRTY?
FROM THE EYES, THIS TIME?!
ZAP ZAP ZAP ZAP
LASERS TOO!
eep...
AS IF THAT WOULD WORK!
BONK
URK.
ARGH!
BLINK BLINK BLINK
I'VE ALSO GOT AN EYE ATTACK ♡
YOO HOO ♥

BRO-
BOT
BEAM!
ZADOOOM
AAAHHH~!
NOT EVEN MARIO AND BOWSER CAN BEAT A BATTLE ROBOT, I SUPPOSE.
BROBOT MISSILE!
EYE LASER!
eeek~!
ZAP ZAP ZAP
KABOOOM
AAHH!
ZAP
KABOOM
ARGH!
ENOUGH OF ALL THIS...
... LUIGI!
PERSISTENT, AREN'T YOU? BUT I'M NOT THIS LUIGI PERSON!
YOU'RE MY...
MY...
YOU DEFINITELY ARE!
MARIO!
BOING

KAPOW
MY DEAR LITTLE BROTHER!
NOOOO!
LUIGI!
TURN BACK TO NORMAL!
BWOOP
WHAT'D YOU EXPECT?
ARGH.
THAT SMARTS.
FLING
I GUESS I'M EATING THIS ONE!
KADOOM

LUIGI! IT'S CUZ I'VE GOT YOU AROUND...
... THAT I TRY SO HARD!
I NEED YOU!
SO COME BACK TO ME, LUIGI!
WE'RE THE BEST BROS IN THE WHOLE UNIVERSE!
POW
POW
POW
FLASH
ZAAP
SILENCE!
AAAH?!
LOOK, THE PURE HEART!
SPARKL
SPARKL
SPARKL
SOME-THING'S RAINING DOWN!
THOSE ARE...

WHAT IS THIS?!
OOH!
LOTS OF FLOWERS... WITH COINS!
BROBOT VANISHED!
ZWOO—OP
THE PURE HEART RESPONDED TO MARIO'S OWN PURE HEART...AND GAVE US THIS GIFT!
Thank you.
LUIGI IS HIMSELF AGAIN!
BIG BRO!
COINS, COINS, COINS.
STOP IT, YOU!

HAPPY FLOWER !
AN ITEM SURE TO MAKE EVERYONE HAPPY!!
Foiled again, said Count Bleck.
LUIGI !
WAHHH!
BIG BRO! I MISSED YOU!
FS—H
FIFTH PURE HEART: ACQUIRED!! AFTER MUCH EFFORT! ♡
HAPPY.
MY TURN NEXT!
HUH ?
DID I DO SOMETHING WRONG?!
BOP
BOP
BOP
YOU RAN ME THROUGH THE WRINGER!

STAGE 6
WHO'S THE FOURTH HERO?!

Hero #1
BAM
MARIO !!
WHEN THE FOUR HEROES OF LIGHT COME TOGETHER, THE WORLDS WILL BE SAVED FROM DESTRUCTION.
-THE LIGHT PROGNOSTICUS
Hero #2
BAM
BOWSER !!
WHAP
WRONG OUTFIT, YOU!
AHH !
Hero #3
BAM
LUIGI !!
BAM
Hero #4
TIPPI !!

*This chapter is based on the **Super Paper Mario** game.

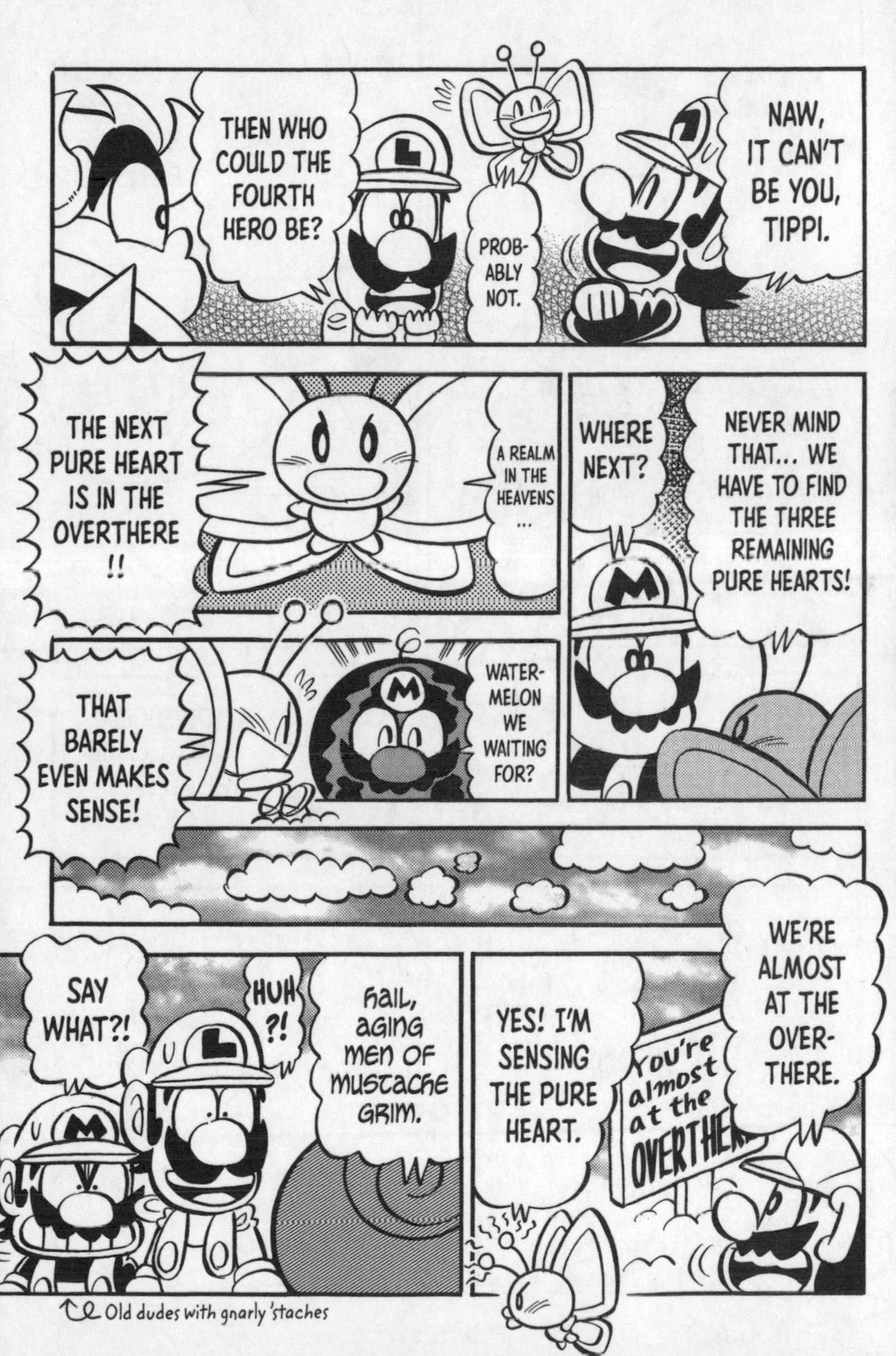
NAW, IT CAN'T BE YOU, TIPPI.
PROB-ABLY NOT.
THEN WHO COULD THE FOURTH HERO BE?
NEVER MIND THAT... WE HAVE TO FIND THE THREE REMAINING PURE HEARTS!
WHERE NEXT?
A REALM IN THE HEAVENS ...
THE NEXT PURE HEART IS IN THE OVERTHERE !!
WATER-MELON WE WAITING FOR?
THAT BARELY EVEN MAKES SENSE!
WE'RE ALMOST AT THE OVER-THERE.
You're almost at the OVERTHE
YES! I'M SENSING THE PURE HEART.
Hail, aging men of mustache grim.
HUH ?!
SAY WHAT?!
Old dudes with gnarly 'staches

VERILY, I PINE FOR A PRINCE. ART THOU THE ONE I HAVE SO LONGED TO MEET? ♡

MY NAME IS LUVBI.

SZZL~~~

MEAT

DID I REQUEST A BEEFY PRINCE? I THINK NOT!

MEAT, YOU SAY ...?

WHO'RE YOU, EXACTLY?

I DESPAIR TO SEE A FACE SO BEHAIRED.

OVERTHERE PRINCESS *LUVBI*

WHY'S THAT?

I WOULD RATHER NOT. HMPH.

YOU SHOULD HEAD BACK TO WHEREVER IT IS YOU CALL HOME.

LET'S GET LUVBI BACK HOME, BRO.
WE DON'T HAVE TIME FOR THAT!
THE PURE HEART IS WAITING FOR US.
Hey!
AND THE SUPER MARIO GALAXY GAME IS AROUND THE CORNER.
Yukio

I CAN JUST CARRY HER LIKE THIS.
ON-WARD, MY STEED! ♡
FINE. WE'LL GET YOU HOME.
Huzzah! ♡

WHAT'S THE OVERTHERE LIKE?
WARM, PEACEFUL... VERILY, AN IDYLLIC PLACE.
I STILL DESPISE THINE MUSTACHE, THOUGH.
YEAH. WE GET IT.

I CAN SEE THE TOWN.
WE ARRIVE!
GREAT. LET'S GET GOING!....
THE OVERTHERE
WAIT. THIS REALM ...

KA-SHNK
IT'S ALL FROZEN !
!
WHAT HAPPENED HERE?
MICRO-WAVE TIME.
THEY'RE NOT FROZEN MEALS!
I WISH WE COULD ASK SOMEONE, BUT THEY'RE ALL ON ICE.
AHH !
What hath trans-pired here?!
Lady Luvbi! Terrible news!
Monsters hath attacked ...
LEAVE THE ICE MELTING TO ME.
MELTING ISN'T BURNING!
BWOOOM
AAAHH~!

LUIGI! DON'T GET INVOLVED!
WHY DID THESE MONSTERS ATTACK?
AGREED...
We're busy.
SOUNDS LIKE TROUBLE WE DON'T NEED! LET'S SPLIT.
WHAM
LET'S GET INVOLVED, LUIGI!
AHH!
THE MONSTERS ARE SAID TO BE AFTER THE PURE HEART...
Quick 180, there!
FS—H
IN. HIS. SHRINE!
ENSHRINED? HE'S DEAD?!
HUH?
THY FATHER...? THE KING IS IN HIS SHRINE...
WHERE HATH FATHER GONE?
WHAT KINDA MONSTERS?
WHERE'S THE PURE HEART?!
Can we put off my dead-line?
YUKIO
Dead-line?
ONE AT A TIME, PLEASE!
WAIT UP, LUVBI! WE'RE COMING TOO!
I SHALT SALLY FORTH TO YONDER SHRINE!

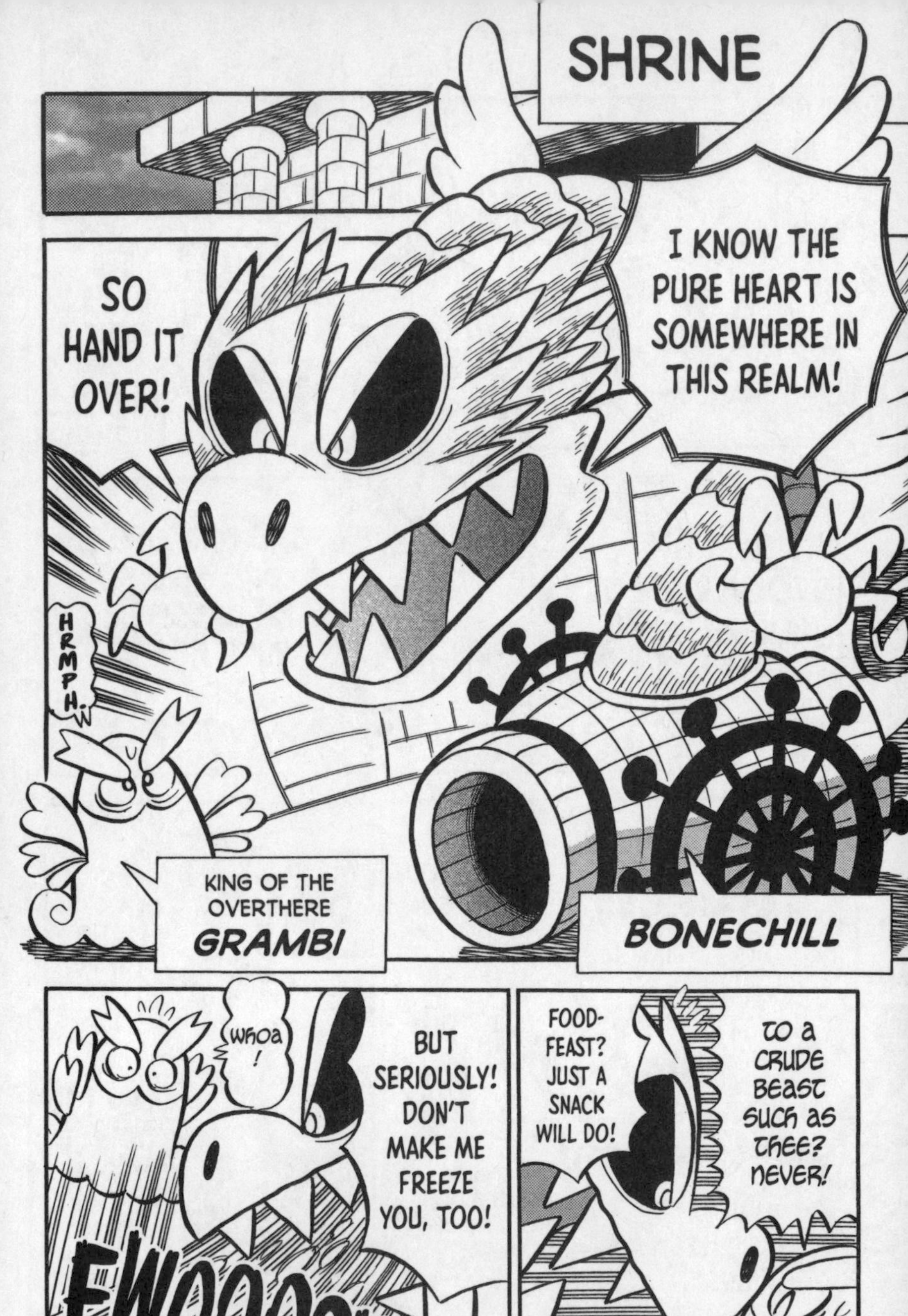
SHRINE
I KNOW THE PURE HEART IS SOMEWHERE IN THIS REALM!
SO HAND IT OVER!
HRMPH...
KING OF THE OVERTHERE GRAMBI
BONECHILL
BUT SERIOUSLY! DON'T MAKE ME FREEZE YOU, TOO!
WHOA!
FWOOOSH
FOOD-FEAST? JUST A SNACK WILL DO!
TO A CRUDE BEAST SUCH AS THEE? NEVER!

THE POWER OF THE PURE HEART WILL MAKE ME YET EVIL-ER!
THOU MAKEST A CONVINCING ARGUMENT FOR NOT GIVING IT TO THEE!

BOP
GIVE IT!
NEVER, FIEND!
LUVBI!
STAY-EST AWAY!
BOP
BOP
FATHER!
FSH
LUVBI?!
PRINCESS OF THIS REALM?

WHAT FUN! I GUESS I'LL FREEZE YOUR DAUGHTER FIRST!
FWOUSH
LUVBI!
WOOSH
RAAAHHH!

FATHER !!
OHH, FATHER !
THOU HAST SACRI-FICED THYSELF FOR ME!
THUD
KASH—NK
AND WHO ARE YOU LOT?!
YOU UGLY JERK!
WHAT A SCUM-BAG.
WE'RE TOO LATE!
WHOOSH
IGNORING US, HUH ?!
PERHAPS THE GIRL KNOWS WHERE THE PURE HEART IS.
Tell me, already!
Wahh !
JUST SOME HEROES ...
...WHO HAPPENED TO BE PASSING BY!
BAM

ENOUGH NOISE!
YEAH!
FIRST, WE'VE GOT SOME MONSTER BUTT TO KICK!
THE PURE HEART COMES LATER.
FWOOOSH
CHILL BLAST!
eeek!
WAHH!
WHOOPS!
CHILL BLAST!
BEATEN SO EASILY?
KA-SHNK
B-BRO...
FWOOSH
eek!
NOT AGAIN!
KA-SH-NK
USE YOUR FIRE! PLEASE!!
PSSS
I'LL MELT YA!
DRIP

FWOOOM
FIRE BLAST!
THANKS.
DRIP
FWOOSH
CHILL BLAST!
URK!
KA-SH~NK
FWOOOM
Phew.
FIRE BLAST!
DRIP
CHILL BLAST!
FWOOSH
FWOOSH
CHILL BLAST!
NOT AT THE SAME TIME! C'MON!!
FWOOOM
FIRE BLAST!
KA-SH~NK
AHHH~!
KA-SH~NK
ARGH!
MIND THY-SELVES, AGED 'STACHE-MEN!
HUH?!
ALL RIGHT... LET'S GET HIM!
UH-HUH!
YEAH!
TOMP TOMP TOMP

YWSH
YWSH
THUNK
WAHH!
ICI-
CLES
!
YOU CAN'T
HOPE TO
MEASURE UP
TO ME!
YWSH
THUNK
eep!!
THUNK
NOOOO!
SHOOM SHOOM
WAHH
!
WE'RE
FINISHED
...
SHOOM SHO-O-OM
ICY
SHARD
STORM
!
THIS
WILL END
YOU!
WHO IS
THAT?!
REFLECTING
MY ICE
SHARDS?
THUD
THUD
THUD
THUD
PARA-
SOL
SHIELD!
BWAM

THE FOURTH HERO OF LIGHT!
PRINCESS PEACH!
SHE'S THE FOURTH!
FWP
YAY!
YOU'RE OKAY!
GETTING HERE WASN'T EASY.
YAY! YAY!
YAY!
THANK GOOD-NESS.
LONG LIVE PEACH!
AHEM ...
AHEM.
SAVE THE SWEET REUNION FOR AFTER THE BATTLE, OKAY?
OH! RIGHT, WE DIDN'T BEAT THIS GUY YET.
WHAT A ROTTEN JERK.
NOW THAT PRINCESS PEACH IS HERE, WE'VE GOT A MILLION TIMES MORE POWER!
WE CAN'T LOSE!
TAKE THAT! AND THAT!
ARGHH!
WHAK
BOP
SMAK
POW
KRAK

Long live Peach!
THANKS TO YOU, PRINCESS PEACH!
WOO-HOO!
WE DID IT!
B-BUT ...
...HOW?!
THUD
I'VE GOT SOUVENIRS!
PICKED UP THESE TWO PURE HEARTS ALONG THE WAY.
HUH?
AWE-SOME!
SO WE ONLY NEED THE FINAL ONE, SOMEWHERE IN THIS REALM...
THIS PRESENCE I'M FEELING... COULD IT BE LUVBI?!
A little overboard!
VERILY... LUVBI IS, HERSELF, A PURE HEART!
WHAT~?
HUH?
SO AS TO PROTECT THE PURE HEART TILL THE HEROES ARRIVED-ETH-ED, I TRANSFORMED IT INTO THIS FAIR FORM...
FORGIVEST ME, LUVBI...
KNOWEST THAT I LOVE THEE.
FATHER...

LUVBI!
MAN OF MUSTACHE! I OUGHT TO HAVE KNOWN—I AWAITED A HERO ALL ALONG.
BUT THIS BE-ETH THE HOUR OF OUR PARTING... THOU MUST DEPART-ETH WITH YONDER HEROES.
HRM. HRM.
THANK THEE FOR ALL THE PAMPERING!
I LOVE THEE AS WELL, FATHER ♡
FA——DE
YEAH! YOU GOT IT!
PWAH
SAVEST ALL THE WORLDS!
HOW ABOUT I BE YOUR CHILD, TO REPLACE LUVBI?
Hmm?
YECHH! I REFUSE!
AND SO, THE FOUR HEROES WOULD NEXT CONFRONT CASTLE BLECK, TOGETHER!

STAGE 7
GAG BATTLE AT THE EDGE OF SPACE!

*This chapter is based on the **Super Mario Galaxy** game, in which Mario and Luma travel around outer space, searching for Power Stars to fuel the Comet Observatory.

I'M NOT FOLLOWING.
LEAVE THIS MANSION, GO THIS WAY, THAT WAY, THEN A LITTLE BIT TO THE LEFT, AND...
THERE'S ONE IN THE OUTSKIRTS OF THIS AREA.
HUH?
WHERE?
I LOVE THIS GUY. ♡
QUIT IT!
SMOOCH~~
SHLORRRP~~
GOT IT!
REALLY?
THAT'S OUR MARIO.
YEAHHH—!
LET'S-A-GO!
GOOD LUCK, BOYS!
FSHFS——H
HONEY... ISN'T THAT WHERE...
YEP.
THAT LITTLE ONE.
BUT I HAVE A FEELING MARIO CAN HANDLE IT...

HE'S MARIO, AFTER ALL...

WAIT UP, BRO!

NEAR ALL THIS RUBBLE, AT THE EDGE OF SPACE...

YEAH.

THIS SHOULD BE THE SPOT BOO MENTIONED.

I HOPE THERE'S ACTUALLY A POWER STAR HERE...

OH!

THERE!

BOULDERGEIST

JUST LIKE THAT LADY BOO SAID!

FSSH

KADOING

HAAAH!!

SHUNK

WHAT THE ...?!

NO
SHOOOM
WAHHHH!
BOULDERGEIST
ROCKS?!
A WHOLE ROCK MONSTER!
SPLAT

A ROCK MONSTER, THOUGH?
I'M PETRIFIED!! LOSING MY MARBLES!!
I'M QUARRIED SICK!! IT'S DO ORE DIE!!
YOU GOT SOME REAL GEMS THERE!!

WHY ARE YOU PEOPLE HERE?!
F-FOR THE POWER STAR...?

ROAR
THE POWER STAR?
eep!

Sure thing.
WE'RE HEADING HOME, BRO!
IF THAT'S ALL, THEN SCRAM!
OR I'LL CRUNCH AND BREAK YOU!
GOOD TO KNOW IT'S DOING WELL.
Heh.
ONLY TO LOOK AT IT, REALLY.
HE SAID "CRUNCH AND BREAK."
NOT "LUNCH BREAK"!
MUNCH MUNCH MUNCH
AL-MOST DONE.
MY PRECIOUS STAR...
AS LONG AS WE'VE GOT THE POWER STAR.♪
NO PROB-LEM.
LOOOM
HUH ?!
HIS HAND !

SLAAAM
NOT YOURS TO TAKE!
AAAAHHHHH!
WORMP
YEAH, YOU! YOU'RE THE ONLY ONE HERE!
YOU'RE GONNA FIGHT ME?
WHAT'S THE BIG IDEA?
YOU WANNA RUMBLE?!
HOPE YOU'RE READY!
WOOSH
YOU'RE ON!
YEP, THAT'S HOW THIS ALWAYS WORKS!
THE STAR'S YOURS IF YOU CAN BEAT ME.
LET'S-A-GO!

PAPER~~
SCISSORS!
ACK!
I LOSE.
EXCEPT THIS AIN'T A SILLY GAME!
KA-DUM
NOW'S MY CHANCE TO NAB THE STAR!
TMP TMP TMP
WAHH~!!
NOT SO FAST!
OWW~
I'M GONNA FIGHT FAIR AND SQUARE FOR THIS STAR!
LUIGI... DON'T BE SUCH A COWARD!
Unnghh.
BUTT POKE~

RMMMBL—
HERE GOES NOTHING!
NOTHING FAIR ABOUT THAT!
THIS IS WHAT YOU GET!
WAP
KA-BOOM
WEAK.
WAHH!
FACE OFF AGAINST MY HAND!
THUMB WRESTLING, IS IT?!

SKWEEZ
ONE, TWO, THREE, FOUR, FIVE, SIX, SEVEN, EIGHT...
GIVE UP, BRO!
ARGH!
YOU'LL HAVE TO WORK TOGETHER TO BEAT THIS THING.
RIGHT.
C'MON, BRO!

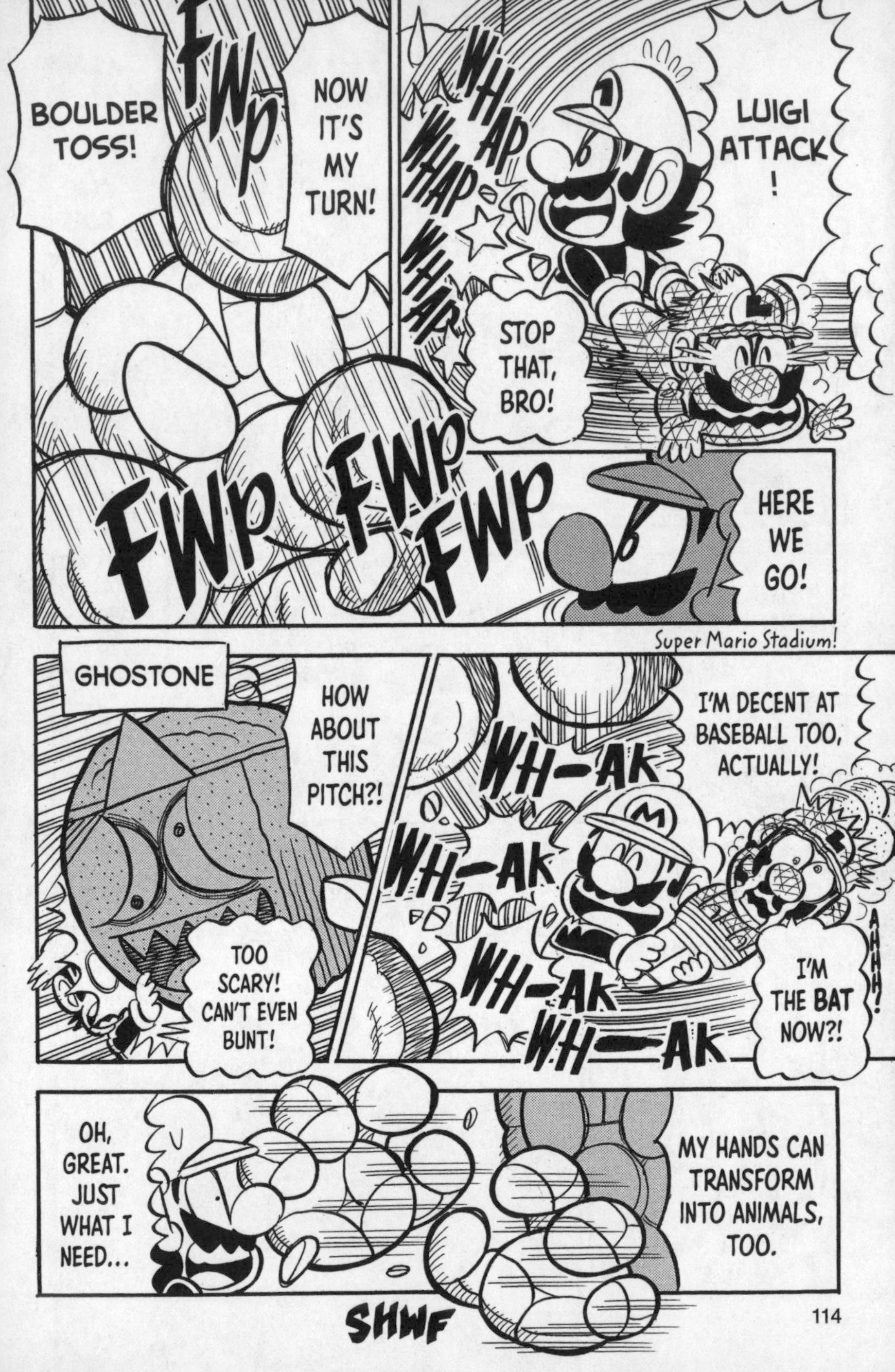
BOULDER TOSS!
FWP
NOW IT'S MY TURN!
WHAP WHAP WHAP WHAP
LUIGI ATTACK!
STOP THAT, BRO!
FWP FWP FWP FWP
HERE WE GO!
Super Mario Stadium!
GHOSTONE
HOW ABOUT THIS PITCH?!
TOO SCARY! CAN'T EVEN BUNT!
I'M DECENT AT BASEBALL TOO, ACTUALLY!
WH-AK WH-AK WH-AK WH-AK
I'M THE BAT NOW?!
AHHH!
OH, GREAT. JUST WHAT I NEED...
MY HANDS CAN TRANSFORM INTO ANIMALS, TOO.
SHWF

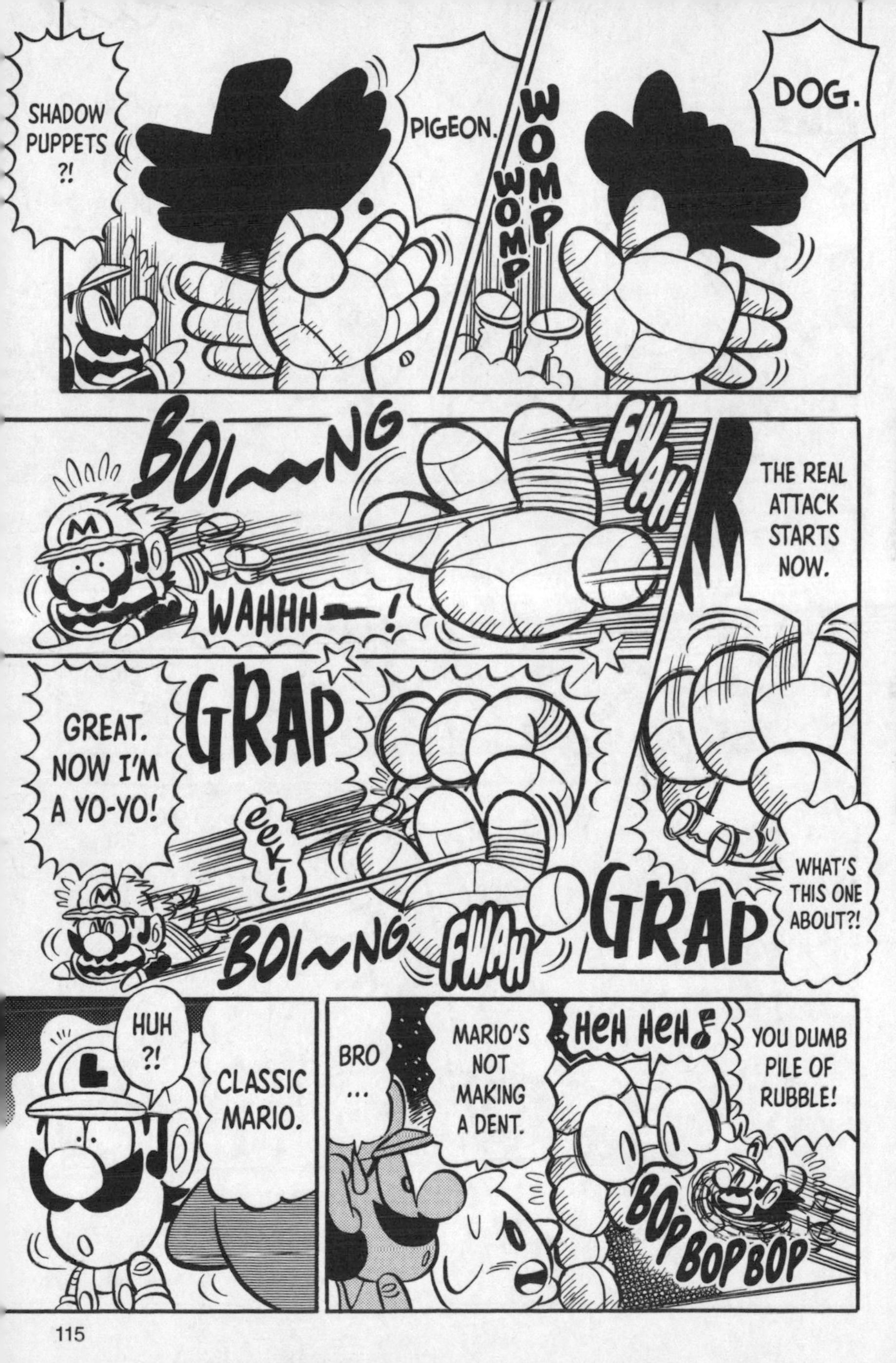
SHADOW PUPPETS ?!
PIGEON.
WOMP WOMP
WOMP WOMP
DOG.
BOI~~NG
FWAH
WAHHH—!
THE REAL ATTACK STARTS NOW.
GREAT. NOW I'M A YO-YO!
GRAP
eek!
BOI~NG
FWAH
GRAP
WHAT'S THIS ONE ABOUT?!
HUH ?!
CLASSIC MARIO.
BRO ...
MARIO'S NOT MAKING A DENT.
HEH HEH♪
YOU DUMB PILE OF RUBBLE!
BOP BOP BOP

IS THAT THE MONSTER'S NAME?!
YES.
BOO!
BOULDER-GEIST... SEEMS TO BE HAVING LOTS OF FUN.
THAT BOY... HE'S A GHOST, JUST LIKE US.
NOT DONE YET!
SPIN ATTACK!
NOT BAD, NOT BAD.
BOP-BOP-BOP-BOP
BUT HE DOESN'T LOOK LIKE THE REST OF US.
LET'S PLAY!
Aaahh!
HE DOESN'T MEAN ANY HARM... BUT HE'S JUST TOO STRONG.
AS TIME PASSED, NOBODY WANTED TO PLAY WITH HIM ANY-MORE.
PLAYING WITH YOU HURTS, GEISTY.
WE JUST CAN'T DO IT.
LET'S GO, GUYS.
ONE BY ONE, HE LOST ALL HIS FRIENDS.

BUT THAT LONELY, ISOLATED GHOST...
NOBODY WANTS TO PLAY.
HMPH. I DON'T NEED FRIENDS.
HE CLOSED OFF HIS HEART AND TOOK UP RESIDENCE HERE, IN THE OUTSKIRTS.
FORE-HEAD...?
GUHH~~!
MORE LIKE FULL-BODY HIT!
WA—K
FORE-HEAD FLICK!
I KINDA DOUBT MY BRO SEES IT THAT WAY.
MARIO IS GETTING HIM TO OPEN UP!
OH!
LOOK! THE ROCKS!
HERE I GO!
YOU READY?
NOW, FOR MY FINAL, ULTIMATE "CRAGGY DANCE."
I'LL TAKE WHATEVER YOU'RE DISHING OUT!
BRING IT ON!

BOULDER-GEIST'S ROCKS ARE ALL HAPPY AND DANCING!
YOU'RE RIGHT! NOW HE'S **ROCKING** OUT!

I'VE NEVER SEEN THIS BEFORE.
BOULDERGEIST IS JUST GLAD MY BRO WANTED TO PLAY WITH HIM.
JUST A LITTLE MORE...
...UNTIL THAT TOUGH STONE ARMOR...
BLAM
...BREAKS AWAY!
AAAHHH!!
WHAM
WHAM
WHAM
WHAM
LOOKS PAINFUL FOR MARIO, THOUGH.

SHAAHH
HIYA, AUNTIE BOO!
YOU'RE FINALLY YOUR TRUE SELF.
BOULDER-GEIST'S TRUE FORM!
THUD THUD THUD THUD
AAHHHH!
YOU CAN LIVE WITH US NOW.
EVERYONE WILL WELCOME YOU.
UH-HUH!
UH-HUH!
THANK YOU, MARIO.
HE'S HERE
GOT... THE STAR.
AWW, THAT'S GREAT.
WHERE'S MARIO?

STAGE 8
THE TALE OF YOSHI AND CHAIN CHOMP
THIS JUMBO RAY LETS US SOAR THROUGH THE SKIES!
DOWN-RIGHT RAY-LAXING!
JUMBO RAY

*This chapter is based on the **New Super Mario Brothers Wii** game, in which Mario and pals travel across various worlds with the help of the flying Jumbo Ray in order to hunt down Bowser's airship and rescue the kidnapped Princess Peach.

LET'S DANGLE SOME BAIT IN FRONT TO MAKE IT GO FASTER.
OKAY!
GREAT IDEA... WHAT'S THE BAIT?
SORRY I ASKED!
MUSH, MUSH!
YUM. ♡
Struggle harder!
WAHH!
I'M NOT A SNACK!
AW!
SURE YOU ARE, YOSHI!
NIP NIP NIP NIP NIP NIP
ZOOOSH
THERE'S THE WORLD 5 CASTLE.
LET'S LAND.
GOOD WORK, JUMBO RAY.
LAND THERE FOR US, OKAY?

KAKRASH KRASH KRASH KRA—SH
AAAHH!
WAHHH!
ACK!
UGH!
KRAK
KRAK
SNAP
SNAP
KRAK
INTO THE CASTLE, THEN...
THIS CASTLE... IS FULL OF METAL SCREENS.
LET'S BE CAREFUL.
ROUGH LANDING, NO?!
Heh.
...MESS AROUND AND GET STUCK IN THEM.
WAH HAHA HAHA
WOMP
WOMP
WOULDN'T WANT TO...
GOOD POINT.

I'M STUCK !
...
GET ME OUTTA HERE!
HELP! PLEASE!
YOU DUMMY!
IF WE MUST.
ONE, TWO ...!
RIP RIP RIP RIP
POP
AAAAHH!!
WOOF~ WOOF~
LOOKS LIKE SOME OTHER DUMMY GOT STUCK TOO.
Heh heh ...
YOU'RE ONE TO TALK!
THAT'S WHAT YOU GET FOR GOOFING OFF.
THAT COULD'VE BEEN A LITTLE GENTLER ...

WORMP
WOOOOF
Wait.
WHO'S THIS?!
IT LOOKS STARVED, BUT...
I THINK THAT'S A CHAIN CHOMP?
WOOF WOOF WHINE
WOOF WOOF WOOF WOOF
IT'S SAYING, "PLEASE HELP ME. I'VE BEEN STUCK HERE FOR A MONTH."
YOU SPEAK CHOM-PESE?
NAH. LET'S BE ON OUR WAY.
WELL, SURE. IT'S A BADDIE.
WOOF~~~
WOOF?!
AHH!
NOPE! I CAN'T RESIST!
SLOW DOWN, YOSHI!

POP
HRNNGH~!!
GRAP
HUH?
YOU CAN EVEN SWALLOW CHAIN CHOMPS ?!
SHLO——OP
THERE. YOU'RE OUT.
WOOF WOOF
AW, YOU WANTED TO HELP.
DON'T DO ANY MORE DUMB STUFF, OKAY?
YOU'RE ONE TO TALK.
HERE, EATING THIS WILL PEP YOU UP.
I CAN EAT ANYTHING, BUT MY FAV IS GOOMBA JERKY.
WOOF~~~!!
CHOMP
Hey!
HURRY IT UP!
Coming!
SEE YA.
WOOF
WOOF

BAM
I'VE BEEN WAITING FOR YOU, YOU CLODS!
WHO'RE YOU CALLING CLODS?!
WAH!
THE BOSS BATTLE STARTED ALREADY?!
WORLD 5 BOSS: *IGGY*

THAT'S ONE SPEEDY ATTACK...
YEAHH!
I'LL HAVE THIS BATTLE FINISHED IN A FLASH!
NOT A CHANCE!
AAHHH!
WHAM
WHAM
WHAM
WHAM
ARGH!
EEK!

HERE. LOOK.

÷ 2 =

THAT'S ALL NON-SENSE!

I COULD BEAT YOU CHUMPS REALLY EASILY, BUT...

...THAT'D BE BORING FOR THE READERS.

SO YOU GET TO FACE MY PET PUP.

GRRR RR~

PET PUP ?!

COME FORTH, GIANT CHAIN CHOMP!

HUGE!

GAH!

WAHH!

ISN'T THAT THE CHOMP FROM BEFORE?
NAW, THAT ONE WASN'T THIS BIG AND SCARY...
THIS DUMMY GOT LOST IN THE CASTLE FOR A WHOLE MONTH, ACTUALLY.
A MONTH?!

WHEN IT FINALLY GOT UN-LOST, I USED MAGIC TO MAKE IT BIG AND STRONG FOR BATTLE!
HMM. I WONDER ...
TOO BAD FOR YOU, IT FOLLOWS MY COM-MANDS.
NOW GET THEM!
WOOF WOOF WOOF WOOF—!!
WHAM
WHAM
WHAM
Gulp.
eep!
AAH!
WAHH!
FIRE-BALL!
EAT THIS!
CHOMP
FWOOP
UM ?!
Ugh

CHAIN CHOMP! BRING IT ON!
RWOOOM
DOUBLE THE FIRE-BACK IN YOUR FACE!
WAS THAT NECES-SARY?
Gah!
WOOF WOOF WOOF
CHOMP CHOMP CHOMP
AAHH!
DO SOME-THING, YOSHI!
CHAIN CHOMP ...
SHAKE!
SPIN
Eep.
TIME FOR A WALK!
WHRL WHRL
WHAM
OWW!
WHAM
WHAM
AAHH!
CHOMP!
NOT WORK-ING!
HMM.
NO WALK! BAD IDEA!
WHAM

ALL ACCORDING TO MY CALCULATIONS!
YOU DUMMIES ARE DONE FOR!
WAH HAHA HAHA HAHA
WHAM
SLAM
GWEHH!
TUMBL TUMBL TUMBL
ACK!
MY SNACK HOARD!
HOW MUCH WERE YOU CARRYING?!
GOOMBA JERKY!
!
WOOF WOOF WOOF
eek!
HERE IT COMES!
Wah!
FSH

IT IS THE CHAIN CHOMP FROM EARLIER!
SLRR~P SLRR~P
SLRR~P
WOOF~ WOOF~ WOOF~
HUH ?!
IT REMEMBERED US!
AH!
WOOF WOOF WOOF WOOF!
ROAR!
AAHH!
ARGH!
CHOMP CHOMP
QUIT IT!
AAAHH!
WOW!
TOO PAINFUL TO WATCH, ALMOST...
YOU GOT YOUR EYES GLUED TO IT!
HUH?
WOOF!!

THANKS, CHAIN CHOMP!
WOOF ~

CALCULA-TIONS CAN'T ACCOUNT FOR SOME THINGS.
UGH ~
WHY, THOUGH ?!

LOOKS LIKE YOSHI SAVED US THIS TIME.
THAT'S RIGHT.

CHAIN CHOMP BIT THE HAND THAT *DIDN'T* FEED IT.
DANG IT.

WOOF WOOF WOOF
NAW, THAT'S JUST A LOVE BITE.
WAHH!
I THINK IT TURNED EVIL AGAIN!

*This chapter is based on the **Super Mario Sunshine** game.

SLA-M

... HAVE A...

HEYA MARIO, LET'S...

OH! YOSHI!

WHAT'S GOING ON WITH HIM?!

HOW RUDE!

YOSHI! YOU'RE STILL HERE ...?

WAIT UP! PLEASE TAKE ME WITH YOU?

LET US BE OFF, MARIO!

YEAH!

SOMETHING'S FISHY, HERE.

WOMP

BUH-BYE!

NAH, YOU SHOULDN'T COME ALONG.

ZOOP~

SEE? IT WORKED.
OH NO, I'VE LOST THEM!
FSHFSH
WE, TOO, ARE OBVIOUS!
TREES.
BLINK
BEING SPOTTED WOULD BE UNFORTU-NATE.
WE JUST GOTTA MAKE SURE YOSHI DOESN'T SPOT US AGAIN.
FS———H

KA-SPLOOSH
AAHH ~~!
THERE ARE MORE OVER HERE!
HAH!
KA-SPLOOSH
GOTCHA, BADDIES!
eek!
HAVE A DRINK!
PLENTY FOR WHAT...? WHERE ARE THEY TAKING THEM?
I AGREE.
GREAT, THAT SHOULD BE PLENTY.
MMM. LOOKS SO YUMMY!
DROOL
NOW IT'S A BUNCH OF FRUIT...?
UGH! HEAVY!
BUT WHY?!
WOMP
CAN'T LET YOSHI FIND ANY OF THIS STUFF.
YES!

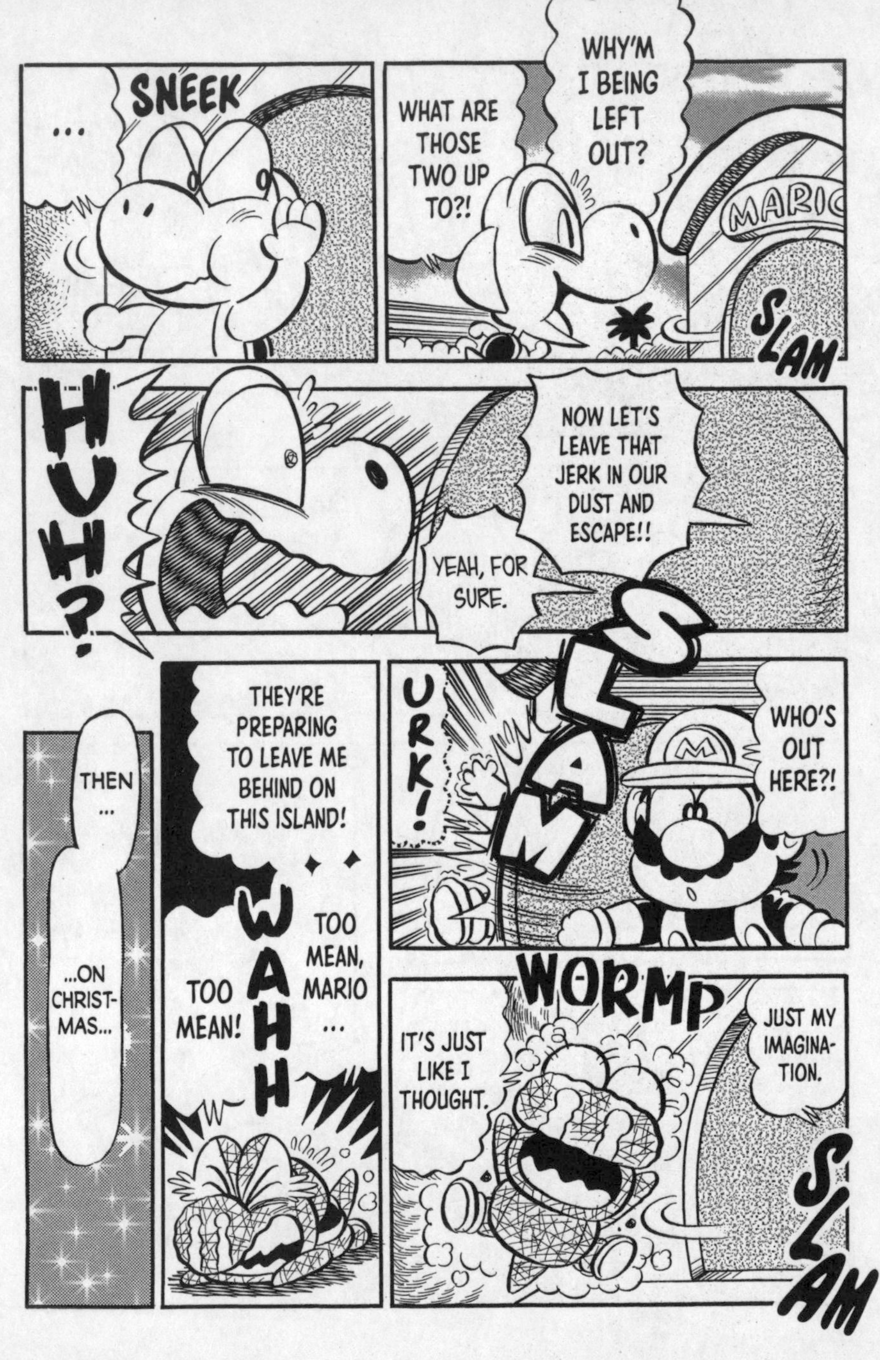
SNEEK
...
WHAT ARE THOSE TWO UP TO?!
WHY'M I BEING LEFT OUT?
MARIO
SLAM
HUH?!
NOW LET'S LEAVE THAT JERK IN OUR DUST AND ESCAPE!!
YEAH, FOR SURE.
SLAM
URK!
WHO'S OUT HERE?!
THEN ...
...ON CHRIST-MAS...
THEY'RE PREPARING TO LEAVE ME BEHIND ON THIS ISLAND!
WAHH
TOO MEAN!
TOO MEAN, MARIO ...
WORMP
IT'S JUST LIKE I THOUGHT.
JUST MY IMAGINA-TION.
SLAM

BAM
MERRY CHRISTMAS YOSHI—
MERRY CHRIST-MAS, YOSHI!
THIS SPECIAL CAKE IS FULL OF SUGAR!
WE MADE IT JUST FOR YOU, YOSHI!
HUH?!

I COULD NEVER EAT ALL THIS ALONE THOUGH...
THANK YOU, MARIO!
Only you can eat this, actually.
Let's leave that jerk in our dust and escape!!
OH, THAT...? WE WERE WATCHING TV AT THE TIME.
OKAAAY!
CHOMP
JUST BE SURE TO SAVOR IT NICE AND SLOW, OKAY?
URRP!
YUMMY!
IN ONE BITE? REALLY?!
URRK.
URK.
YOSHI...
...IS CRYING FROM HAPPINESS.
SALTY CAKE ASIDE, YOSHI'S BELLY WAS FULL OF GOOD CHEER.
HORK~~
HORK.
SUGAR...?
I THINK YOU USED SALT BY MISTAKE!
Ack!

PLEASE READ BEFORE CONTINUING

—NOTE FOR PARENTS—

The stories in the following section deal with the passing of a parent. While this material is still within the ranges of an All Ages rating, it may be upsetting for children who are sensitive to this kind of subject matter.

We opted to include the stories here because they are part of the creator's original greatest hits, which he selected himself. But with permission of the creator, we have moved the stories from where they were placed in the original Japanese volume to the back of this volume.

SPECIAL STAGE
SUPER MARI-OLD
FIRST MY BROTHER DISAPPEARED A MONTH AGO...
AND THEN, ANOTHER DISASTER STRUCK!

TERRIBLE NEWS!
PRINCESS PEACH HAS BEEN KIDNAPPED... FOR THE MILLIONTH TIME!!
WHAAAT?

OF COURSE THIS WOULD HAPPEN WHEN MARIO'S MISSING...

WHAT DO WE DO?

YOU'LL JUST HAVE TO HANDLE IT, LUIGI!

WHO, *ME?!*

I'D BETTER GET A MOVE ON!

TO WHERE, EXACTLY?!

ARE YOU RUNNING AWAY FROM HOME?

HMM...

I SHOULD TAKE THIS TOO!

Poltergust 3000

THERE ARE NO GHOSTS TO VACUUM UP!

TAKE IT EASY, LUIGI!

HUH?
REALLY?!
I KNOW WHERE MARIO IS!
YOSHI?!
HEY, LUIGI!
HMM?
WAAH! I CAN'T TAKE THE PRESSURE!
I'LL TAKE YOU THERE. HOP ON!
TELL US, TELL US!
WHERE IS HE?
WHERE?!
WHERE'S MARIO?!
TA-DA!
THE HOSPITAL?! WHY'S MY BRO HERE...?
MUSHROOM HOS
OH, YOU'LL SEE.
THUD
NOT ALL OF YOU!
Too many Toads...!
JUST LUIGI, PLEASE.

WOMP WOMP
IT'S ...
IT'S-A *YOU,* MARIO!
PEACH, HUH...
RIGHT!
MARIO! PRINCESS PEACH GOT KID-NAPPED! AGAIN!
TELL HIM ABOUT PRINCESS PEACH, LUIGI...
WHAT'S WRONG? HE DOESN'T LOOK SO HOT.
Not even luke-warm ...

PUNS LIKE THAT!
"HOW PUZZLING!"
TOO CORNY!

"KID-NAPPED? I'M SHAT-TERED!"
THAT'S RIGHT. NORMALLY, YOU'D BE LIKE...
SMASH SMASH

YOU DO, MARIO!
WHO DOES THAT?

CHECK OUT MY HANDS ...
HUH?!
NAW, I'M DONE WITH JOKES AND GAGS...

AS USUAL, VERY CLEAR DUMMY AND DINGUS LINES...
DON'T READ MY PALM.
AND WHAT'S A DINGUS LINE ANYWAY?!
MY BACK, MY ARMS...
I'M GETTING OLD.
LOOK. WHAT I'M SAYING IS... AFTER 25 LONG YEARS OF FIGHTING, I'M ALL WORN OUT.

THAT'S WHY I'M HERE, AT THE HOSPITAL.
BRO...
YOUR BODY'S IN BAD SHAPE...?

TRUTH IS, IT'S REALLY MY SPIRIT THAT'S HURTING...
THE TRUTH?!
THE TOOTH?!
SMAK

From the Author:
Sometimes I think about this one comic I wrote long ago...
I worked on it when my father was really sick, in the hospital.
SORRY. KINDA STINKY.
WHOOPS, EVEN STINKIER!
OH BOY, THAT'S STINKY...
Even so, I had no choice but to fill the comic with jokes, gags, and tomfoolery.
"FATHER" ...?!
OKAY, C'MON—NO MORE JOKES. LET'S HEAD IN THERE, OKAY?
IF MY HEAD'S COMING, SO'S MY BODY!
My father ended up passing away.
CUT IT OUT!
HEY, LEAVE MY WIFE ALONE!
HUH ?!
And still I wrote a story about Papa Blooper doing his best...
WE'VE BEEN MARRIED FOR YEARS. SHE'S MY EVERY-THING!
SO I'M GONNA PROTECT HER!
AWW, HONEY ...

Losing my father made me so sad that I ended up in the hospital. Even then, I still had to keep coming up with jokes for the comic.
WAHHH!
IN THIS COMIC, I HAVE TO BE THIS BRIGHT, CHEERY GUY ALL THE TIME...
Sometimes the hardest thing in the world is to be funny.
AH, THAT LOOSENED UP MY SHOULDERS.
GREAT...
BRO, YOU'RE NOT MAKING JOKES OR RIFFING ON OUR GAGS!
AND YOU'RE SAYING SOME STRANGE THINGS...
PLENTY OF JOKES HERE WOULD BEAR FRUIT.
ONLY THE LOW-HANGING KIND...
OVER THE 25 YEARS OF THIS COMIC, PLENTY OF SITUATIONS WERE NO LAUGHING MATTER.
EVEN THEN, I HAD TO KEEP MAKING EVERYONE LAUGH...
BRO...
GRR

WHAT'S WRONG?! DON'T MAKE ME FORCE IT OUT OF YOU!
THIS IS A GAG COMIC! YOU'RE GONNA LOSE YOUR JOB!
WHAP
WHAP
WHAP
LUIGI, THAT WON'T WORK. LET ME TRY.
HE NEEDS AN INJECTION OF JOKE SPIRIT!
PUOOOMP
FSSH FSSH
FSSH FSSH
THAT WON'T WORK EITHER!
KNOCK IT OFF. THESE JOKES ...
THEY'RE NOT HELPING.
FWOOOOO
I'LL NEVER BE A GAG MAN AGAIN.
WOW ...
MARIO ...
WHAT A GLOOMY FELLOW!
HUH ?!

DR. MARIO!

I'LL FIX HIM RIGHT UP!

WHICH ONE'S REAL? HOW CAN WE GET TO THE **TOOTH** OF THE MATTER?!
GAH!
T-TWO OF THEM ?!
YES, YES, I SEE...

TAKE YOUR MEDICINE!

HRRNGH ~~!

THIS STUFF WORKS GREAT!

SHUV SHUV

MMMF!!

CAN I SEE YOUR MEDICAL LICENSE?

GLOMP

THAT'S NOT GONNA CURE MY BRO!

FSHH

KA-SHWING

THE MEDICINE WORKED. ♡

THESE 25 YEARS WEREN'T *ALL* PAIN AND MISERY.

THERE WERE PLENTY OF GOOD TIMES TOO.

THAT'S RIGHT.

...

...

HOW DO YOU KNOW, DR. BRO...?
Yes.
PLENTY OF GOOD TIMES, INDEED.
WELL? TELL US ABOUT THE GOOD TIMES!
Oh, there was lots of fan mail, various events...

WAIT, SO THIS SERIES WILL GO ON FOR ANOTHER 25 YEARS?

HUHHH?

We're in sci-fi terri-tory?

BECAUSE I'M MARIO FROM 25 YEARS IN THE FUTURE, WHEN THIS SERIES IS CELEBRATING ITS 50TH ANNIVERSARY!

YUKIO

I'LL BE 88 YEARS OLD!

I'M FEELING MUCH BETTER.
I'M GLAD THE MEDICINE SEEMS TO BE WORKING SO QUICKLY!
TRUST ME, I KNOW HOW YOU FEEL.
LITERALLY! YOU ARE HIM!
ALL RIGHT, MY WORK HERE IS DONE.
BACK TO THE FUTURE FOR ME!
THAT TIME MACHINE LOOKS A LITTLE FAMILIAR!
MARIO
I had forgotten something important.
THANK YOU, MARIO!
ZWOOP
BE YOU AGAIN, SOME-DAY...
What helps me during the tough times are the jokes and gags.
OH RIGHT, BRO! PRINCESS PEACH GOT KIDNAPPED AGAIN...
YOU DON'T SAY?
TIME TO SAVE HER...

WHEN THERE'S TROUBLE, CAL-A-MARIO! CUZ I CAN'T WAIT TO STIR UP A GOOD FIGHT!
Your smiles and laughs will always do the trick!
YOU GOTTA BE SQUID-DING ME!
STIR STIR STIR
I DID NOT C THIS ENDING COMING!
And this Mario comic will always be all about the gags!
LUIGI'S TEARY COMEBACK
Good luck, Mario! And good luck, me!

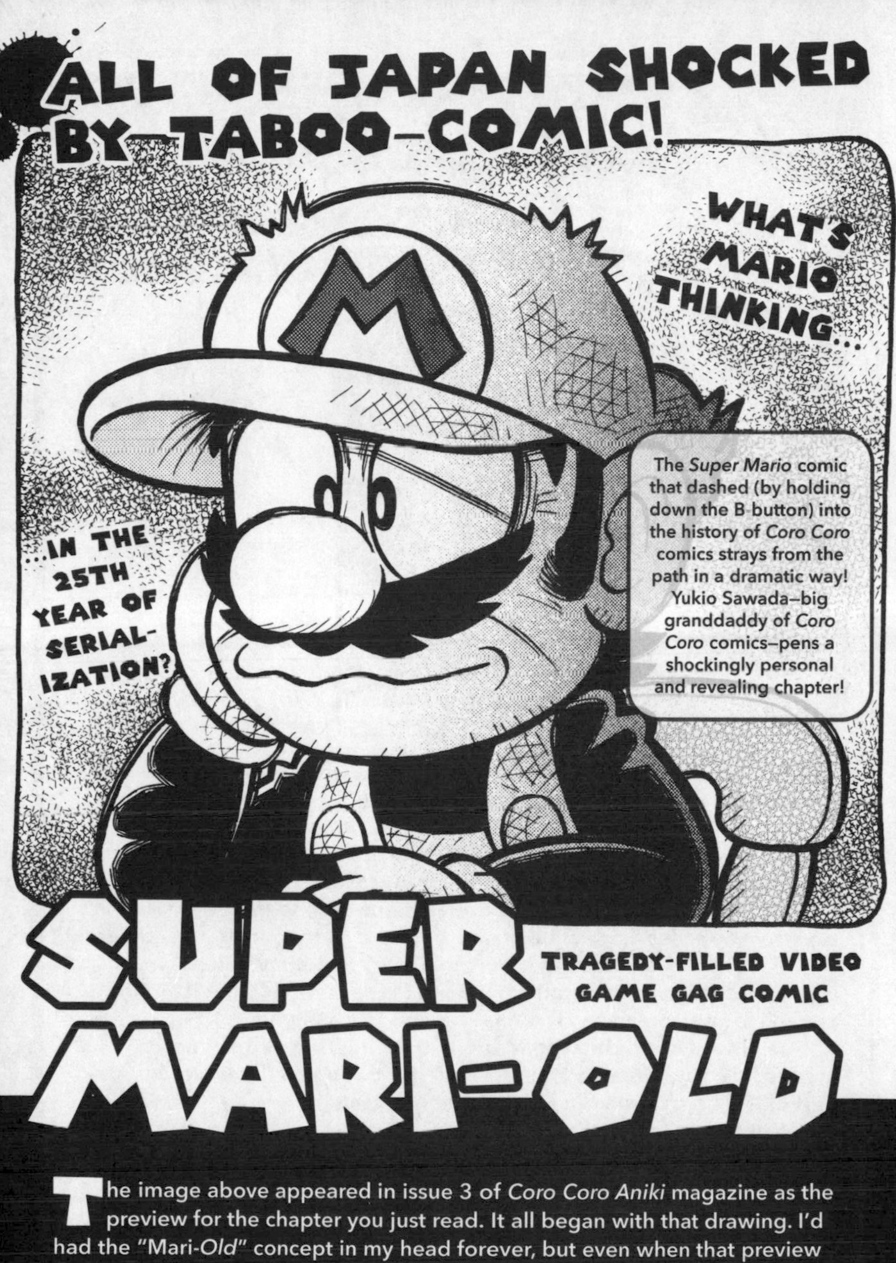

The image above appeared in issue 3 of *Coro Coro Aniki* magazine as the preview for the chapter you just read. It all began with that drawing. I'd had the "Mari-*Old*" concept in my head forever, but even when that preview image came out, I still hadn't worked out most of the story for the upcoming chapter. How should I draw Mario, exactly?! I couldn't come up with an easy answer, so they slapped that "All of Japan Shocked by Taboo Comic!" headline onto the image. The person most shocked by it was *me*.

OLD YUKIO SAWADA'S SUPER SECRETS PART 1

ABOUT SUPER MARI-OLD

My father was given three months to live when he was diagnosed with pancreatic cancer. I was living in Chiba at the time, but the hospital was in Osaka, so I was constantly trekking back and forth. Due to the extreme stress, I came down with face paralysis (Bell's palsy) which left me unable to move the right side of my face.

That was over 15 years ago. When it came time to do the "Mari-*Old*" story for the series' 25th anniversary, I wanted to try portraying a different sort of Mario while including a personal story about my father. I went into a lot detail about my father's health in the first draft, but it wound up feeling way too heavy. The final version is a bit lighter.

I've always loved drawing Mario and friends, but at the time, it was hard to keep up with everything. I only got through it thanks to the support of the *Coro Coro* editorial team and my family.

Sometimes I feel that "Super Mari-*Old*" is just me feeling sorry for myself. Why put something like that out into the world?!

At least, I used to feel that way. I feel differently now. I think it's like when you rant to a friend and end up feeling better? So, thank you for listening.

Despite the subject matter, I had a lot of fun drawing this darker version of Mario, and I'm grateful to Nintendo and *Coro Coro Aniki* for letting me!!

OLD YUKIO SAWADA'S SUPER SECRETS PART 2

This was a piece of art I drew as an apology, since I couldn't attend the "Nintendo x Nico Nico Honsha" *hanafuda* card game tournament on September 24, 2016.

Of course I'd been secretly practicing with my Mario-themed hanafuda card set, but I had a *Monthly Coro Coro* deadline on the horizon that I couldn't neglect. What a shame!

YUKIO SAWADA
2016.9.24
I'm sorry I couldn't attend today! As an apology, please accept this gag!
Look, it's Hanaporka Mario.
SNORT
You're hogging the spot-light!

My favorites in that Mario-themed hanafuda set are January's Baby Mario and February's Yoshis. And from the Club Nintendo set, I'm fond of August's Boo and November's Princess Peach w/Parasol.

NICO NAMA HANAFUDA TOURNEY

AND NOW, THE AFTERWORD

I often get asked, "You're really still doing the *Super Mario-kun* manga?"

This year marks the 27th year of serialization*, yes. We're almost at 28.

I never imagined it would go on this long!

More than anything, I'm grateful to the readers of this series.

I once had a dad come up to me at a meet-and-greet, and he said, "Two different generations, myself and my kids, now both read your manga!" Nothing could make me happier than hearing that.

That makes sense, though, since readers who started at age ten would be 37 now.

It all started when I imagined how *Yoshimoto Shinkigeki* (a comedy show I love) would approach the *Mario* canon.

* This afterword was written in 2017, when the Japanese edition of this volume was first published.

I added a bunch of elements from the actual games, and that's how *Super Mario-kun* came into being.

Twenty-seven years later, is that approach still working?

Can I still have fun and mess around on the same level as the little kids who are reading my series?

I'm not as spry as I used to be, so maybe the *Super Mario-kun* manga will end when my body fails me.

For now, I'm aiming to power through for at least three more years and reach that coveted 30th anniversary.

I have a four-year-old grandchild, so maybe they'll be a reader too, three years from now.

ABOUT THE AUTHOR

YUKIO SAWADA was born on March 12, 1953, in Osaka, Japan. He made his debut in 1980 with *Notteru Hero-kun* (Hero-kun on the Move) in Tokuma Shoten's *T.V. Land* magazine.

He is most known for his long-running series *Super Mario-kun* (Shogakukan), currently serialized in *Coro Coro Comics* and *Coro Coro Ichiban*. He is also the manga creator of *Super Mario Brothers 2* (Tokuma Shoten), *Ore da-yo! Wario da-yo!!* (It's Me! Wario!!) (Shogakukan), and many other series. Sawada was the recipient of the 65th Shogakukan manga award in 2020.